The Ghost of Rockcove Hall

There was a creak in the wall beside my bed. And then I heard it. The sound, so infinitesimal, that I had recognized for the first time, earlier, as a footstep on a stair tread in the wall.

The intruder wasn't coming by foot or sea. The intruder was already here. Had been here, perhaps, all along...

The steps climbed upward, moved across the ceiling in the attic crawl space, and disappeared in the direction of the hall's central core. I knew suddenly where they were going.

I reached for the telephone to call Paul, and the line was dead. . . .

The Watcher
in the Mist

by Norma Johnston

BANTAM BOOKS
TORONTO · NEW YORK · LONDON · SYDNEY · AUCKLAND

RL 6, IL age 12 and up

THE WATCHER IN THE MIST
A Bantam Book / October 1986

*Starfire and the accompanying logo of a stylized star are
registered trademarks of Bantam Books, Inc. Registered in U.S.
Patent and Trademark Office and elsewhere.*

*Bantam Books are published by Bantam Books, Inc. Its trade-
mark, consisting of the words "Bantam Books" and the por-
trayal of a rooster, is Registered in U.S. Patent and Trademark
Office and in other countries. Marca Registrada. Bantam
Books, Inc., 666 Fifth Avenue, New York, New York 10103.*

PRINTED IN THE UNITED STATES OF AMERICA

O   0 9 8 7 6 5 4 3 2 1

The Watcher
in the Mist

One

The airlines terminal, even at midday, was hectic. I shouldn't be surprised, I thought, looking around me with a rush of exhilaration. Yet, actually, everything was surprising—most of all the fact that here I was, Cindy Clayborne, arriving alone at Logan Airport, Boston, while the rest of my family was by now somewhere over the Atlantic.

Here I was, but where was Elizabeth? My distant cousin, now my employer for the summer, had promised she'd be here waiting when I emerged from the New York Air arrival tube. But I'd already waited fifteen minutes, and there was no sign of her.

I was sure I'd recognize Elizabeth even though it was six years since I'd seen her last. I'd been eleven the year the Lancasters had come down from Boston to spend Christmas with us in New Jersey. Now I was seventeen. Elizabeth was about to turn Rockcove Hall, the Lancaster family homestead on Cape Ann, into an inn, with me there as the waitress and mother's helper. And Elizabeth's husband, Dan Lancaster, whom I vaguely remembered as big, warm, and humorous, was dead.

Elizabeth, I remembered better. Elizabeth, with her classic features, dark hair and honey-colored skin, and her deep serenity, had seemed like Cinderella and the fairy godmother rolled into one. But there was no one remotely like that in the New York Air waiting area. There was no one, even, whose upheld cardboard sign said C. CLAYBORNE. If I waited much longer, there'd be nobody here at all.

And meanwhile, my luggage was probably going around and around on a carousel somewhere. My father had given me firm instructions about retrieving my luggage promptly. It had taken a lot of arguments, persuasion, and a few tears to get my parents to let me fly alone. It was almost as hard as convincing them to let me take a summer job away from home instead of going to Europe with them and my younger brother. I'd never have succeeded if Elizabeth hadn't needed me so much.

That was the point I'd stressed during the past three weeks, not mentioning that actually I dreaded the prospect of trailing my parents through museums (my father's been known to spend a half hour inspecting a single object). Not mentioning that Bill Rhodes, whom I'd adored from afar for the past three years, and only recently dated for the first time, just happened to have a summer job in Gloucester, exactly eight and a quarter miles from Rockcove Hall.

"Elizabeth needs me! She's your second cousin, Mother, and you used to be like sisters, and this is the first time she's ever asked anything of us. I *want* to help her!" That's what I'd argued so persuasively. And it hadn't been a lie, even if it had not been *all* the truth.

Bill Rhodes hadn't been all the rest of it either. There had been something I'd sensed between the lines of Elizabeth's letter, behind her words when she spoke to us on the phone. Something that Mother, for all their childhood closeness, had apparently not noticed... and that I, even though I needed strong reasons to persuade my parents, hadn't mentioned. A feeling that Elizabeth didn't need just help, she needed *me*. A feeling that somewhere beneath her surface serenity something was gravely wrong.

Now, standing alone in the cool gray light of the airport, I shuddered. Then I shook the shudder off and laughed. My imagination was too active just as Dad always told me. Elizabeth was probably waiting down by the luggage carousel. I picked up my heavy carry-on bag and followed signs to the luggage area.

There was no one at all waiting there—only my two soft-sided suitcases riding forlornly around and around. I pulled them off the carousel, looked vainly for a luggage cart, and began dragging them toward the information desk. I'd brought a lot because I'd be here all summer. And, of course, Elizabeth was going to meet me....

There was no message for me at the information desk. There was no sign of Elizabeth at the passenger pick-up door as the young woman at the information desk suggested. At least I found an empty luggage cart. I loaded it and pushed it back inside to the nearest bank of telephones.

Fortunately I'd kept Elizabeth's phone number in my purse. The phone rang and rang. Elizabeth was probably on her way here and had brought the children. But all the time an uneasiness was growing in the bottom of my stomach. I was about to hang up, when I heard the phone almost fall off its hook on the other end.

"*Hello!*" The voice, breathless and frantic, was ten-year-old Lissa's.

"Lissa?" Unconsciously I spoke rapidly myself. "Lissa, it's Cindy. Cindy Clayborne. Where's your mother? She was going to meet—"

"I know! She couldn't go. She said if you called— tell you—" Lissa swallowed. "Mom says you're to take the train to Rockport. It goes from North Station in Boston. She says the people in the airport can tell you how to get there."

The phone went dead.

The information clerk, eyeing my luggage dubiously, told me the train station was on the other side of town and I'd probably be smart to take a taxi. By now it was after two and I was not only worried, I was starved. But I turned my back resolutely on the terminal's cheerful coffee shop. Better wait till I reached the train station, since I had no knowledge of the schedule.

I went out into a burst of Boston heat. The glass door gave me back a discouraging reflection. My prized pale linen suit was a rumpled mess; my chestnut-colored hair had lost its blow-dried curve and hung, bedraggled. I thought longingly of the swimming pool Elizabeth had spoken of, the swimming pool Dan had promised her when he'd inherited Rockcove Hall and they'd moved there from Boston as full-time residents two years before. Only the pool hadn't been finished in time for that first summer, and last year Dan had died in a boating accident as summer first began.

He didn't die. He was killed. Dan Lancaster grew up on boats; he spent every summer from birth to law school at Rockcove Hall. He was killed in an accident when he took his boat out into the very teeth of a storm.

I jerked myself up sharply. Where had those words come from, bursting suddenly into my thoughts?

"Hey, girlie! You standing there looking for your boyfriend, or you want a cab?" The cab stood in front of me, its passenger door open, and the cabbie was waiting with obvious impatience. Blushing, I piled inside.

North Station was big, barnlike, and bleak. There was no place to eat, no rest rooms, and the train would not arrive for another hour. I'd seen a fast-food place across the street, but the thought of dragging my suitcases through those multiple lanes of traffic was too daunting. I sat and waited, telling my stomach to have the decency to keep quiet. But I couldn't discipline my thoughts.

What had happened to Elizabeth? Why had Lissa sounded so upset? Why hadn't Elizabeth gotten in touch with me? Stop it, I told myself sternly. Elizabeth had left instructions for me with Lissa, so nothing could be too awfully wrong. Clearly she had confidence in my self-reliance.

The realization buoyed me till the Cape Ann train was announced. A long, jostling line pushed out to the train platform, and there were no porters, no luggage carts. I shoved my suitcases ahead of me grimly, cursing beneath my breath. The two nearest cars were so full that their doors had been closed. I hesitated at the next car, uncertain.

"Go on!" an impatient voice said behind my ear.

I looked around. A young man a few years older than me pushed at my shoulders, scowling. Maybe he didn't push deliberately; maybe it was the crowd behind that caused him to lurch forward. But there was no mistaking the irritation in his voice. "Are you taking the train or aren't you?" he demanded. Without waiting for my answer he seized my suitcases, swung them up the steps, and set them inside the car.

"Thank you," I muttered coldly.

"I wasn't trying to pick you up. Just to get you out of my way," he retorted just as icily. He pushed on through the crowded aisle, leaving me more scarlet than ever, and not from Boston heat.

I squeezed myself into the one remaining empty seat near the door. More people piled in—commuters, vacationing families, kids wearing bathing suits and carrying radios that were on full blast. The car doors slammed shut, the engine belched, and the train got under way. Three couples packed into two facing double seats behind me were eating pizza, and the smell nauseated me.

The train jerked to a stop for the third—or was it the fourth—time? The loudspeaker cleared its throat. "*North* Salem! *Last* stop. *Change* for buses to stops beyond."

"But I'm going to Rockport!" I blurted out. "I thought the train went there!" I didn't think anyone heard me. People were pushing past me, racing toward battered buses parked on gravel. I stumbled to my feet and groped for my suitcase handles.

"Go *on!*" It was that voice again. "I'll bring them. You run ahead and grab two seats," he ordered.

Practicality triumphed over pride. I obeyed. The nearest buses were already filled, but the farthest had empty seats behind the driver. Moments later my rescuer pushed in behind me. "Why you women have to cart so much junk on vacations," he said sarcastically, loading my suitcases overhead. "What do you think this is, the South of France?"

I scowled at him, eyeing his grease-smeared jeans pointedly as he sprawled in the seat beside me. His eyes suddenly went very cold.

"I work for a living. Sorry if that offends your highness."

"So do I. Work, that is. That's why I'm here." Why was I telling him that? I regretted it at once, the more so as his eyes traveled over me, top to bottom and up again. Not as if they were undressing me, something almost worse—as if they were measuring me and found me wanting. I turned away from him, toward the window. The bus lurched out of the siding, through the shabby outskirts of the town, and onto the road along the north coast.

Past clumps of gracious houses. Past motels. Past businesses of all sizes and descriptions. The bus windows were open, and the breeze brought the smells of car exhaust and salt and fish. My stomach contracted.

"Want an apple?" It was my neighbor, in a considerably less cantankerous tone. Pride fought with hunger, and my hunger won.

"Thanks." The apple was tart and sweet, bringing back memories of that holiday Elizabeth and

Dan had spent with us. Dan had told stories of his childhood summers on Cape Ann while I showed Lissa how to make apple-clove pomanders, and Elizabeth had watched, laughing.

Beside me, my companion had produced another apple and sunk his teeth into it. "Where in Rockport are you going to work?" he asked.

I could so easily have told him, but I didn't. Something—dignity, self-preservation, a sort of early warning system—made me turn away. And after a moment, with an anger I could feel, he, too, pulled away.

Two

He left the bus in Gloucester. I rode on, and the number of passengers dwindled as the bus snaked through the narrow twisting roads that led to Rockport. Down past Bearskin Neck with its crowds of tourists, around Dock Square and up again past art galleries and shops and guest houses in weathered woods, their prim New England architecture softened by rambling roses. There were flowers everywhere, and people. The bus pulled in at last by railroad tracks that ran between a tiny shopping center and tourist homes. I dragged my suitcases off after me and looked around.

The station area was empty, and the other travelers quickly scattered. I stood, helpless, in the tan pebbles beneath a pitiless late afternoon sun, with no car, no taxi, and no telephone. That was when I realized two things. I was on my own, totally alone—no Elizabeth here to rescue me, as I only now realized I'd expected. And whatever I'd sensed was wrong, troubled, mystifying behind Elizabeth's appeal to me was very wrong indeed.

Somehow, a surge of energy shot through me

alongside the fear. I dragged my suitcases across the tracks into the IGA supermarket. The girl at the service desk was sympathetic. "There's no use calling for a cab. The old man who owns it only works when he feels like it, and never on weekends. You'll just get his answering machine. Where you going?"

"Rockcove Hall."

Did I imagine it, or did something change in her manner? Her eyes looked frankly curious. But she said only, "That's about two miles out. Turn left on Granite Street and you can't miss it." She glanced at my luggage skeptically. "You could try to hitch a ride."

I knew I wouldn't. I went out again into the white glare of sun, and again an odd courage took over in me. After I had gone a block, I found myself turning in to one of the blue-gray cottages that bore a neat white sign. CASTELL GALLERY. I said to the pleasant woman who approached me, "I'm sorry, my name is Cindy Clayborne and I'm on my way to my cousin Elizabeth Lancaster at Rockcove Hall. I can't manage my suitcases without a cab, so I want to leave them here and send a car back for them later."

And I walked out and left them there before the woman could do more than nod, her expression registering her surprise. I turned onto Granite Street again, feeling immeasurably lighter. My face was stinging from the heat, and my feet felt swollen, but as the business area fell behind me, the air grew fresh.

The road wound along the coast, providing glimpses, between scattered houses, of the ocean framed by pines and rocks. To my right, behind

me, was the curving arm of Bearskin Neck, where
long ago a bear had been washed up in a storm.
Out in the harbor, boats with white sails skimmed
proudly in the breeze. A lighthouse, small islands,
buoys with blinking lights. Ahead of me the shoreline curved right again, with gracious houses, and
high on a thrusting point of rock a white building
gleamed in the slanting rays of the sun. I stopped,
arrested.

Had I dreamed that house, or seen its picture?
It could have come out of a history book. The
black roof rose to a widow's walk, all filigree
against the sky. "Widow's walks," Mother had told
me once when I was researching a school report
on the whaling industry. "Those are the rooftop
decks from which the captains' wives used to
watch for their husbands' ships to come home from
sea. Always afraid the ship would not return; that
they'd be widowed. That all the family wealth
would be lost, with their menfolk, in the ocean
deeps."

Below the roof the house rose three stories tall,
but it rambled, as though wings had been added
on. It rambled primly, in disciplined New England
fashion. Red flowers bloomed like bright flags in
hanging baskets, and more flowers ran, in a kalei-
doscopic garden border, down to the rocks. Phlox,
foxglove, liatris, lily, lupine. My mind knew their
names, although I could not see them. For a
second I stood, immobile as a ship's figurehead, as
a strange sensation of having gone back through
time assailed me. Then a car motor roared behind
me, sending a shiver up my spine to break the
spell.

The car slowed, and a familiar voice called out,

"Cindy?" I spun around. Elizabeth, at the wheel of a dark car, leaned out to me. I ran to her, tumbling into the seat beside her.

"Cindy, I'm so sorry. Lissa should have explained, but she was still too scared."

"What happened?" I demanded, slamming the car door behind me. Elizabeth's eyes were somber, though she still had that magical warm huskiness in her voice.

"We had a fire in the kitchen. Not serious, but enough damage that I had to run up to Beverly to pick up replacement pieces or we'd have no stove. And I have a private catering job for Sunday. If only Paul had been around—" She broke off, pressing her lips together tightly, then smiled at me. "What's happened to your luggage?"

"I left it at the Castell Gallery. I'm afraid I didn't give the lady time to say no."

Elizabeth swung the car around to head back. "You run in for them, will you, please? I don't want to stop to talk."

Mrs. Castell was busy with a client. I signaled that I was reclaiming the luggage, and she nodded. Then I was back in the car, and we were speeding up the coast road.

"What kind of fire?" I demanded.

"Some sort of short circuit in the wiring." Elizabeth frowned, not taking her eyes off the road. "Thank God we found it quickly. We wouldn't have if Lissa hadn't happened to go inside to get a cold drink for herself and Kevin. We were all out on the side lawn pulling weeds out of the terrace."

"Where was the staff?"

"There isn't any staff yet, just a woman who comes in to cook, and another to wait tables when we've booked a special party. The inn won't officially open till Fourth of July weekend. Meanwhile there's just us, and Dan's brother, Paul. When he's around."

"He wasn't there today?"

"He's up in Maine. On business." Elizabeth sighed. "Frankly, when I decided to go into business as an innkeeper, I thought I was going to be able to rely on Paul. At least for this first summer. But now he has this idea of salvaging Dan's boat and using it for charters."

Which meant his time would not be at Elizabeth's disposal. It also meant something more. Dan had died in an accident with his boat. I thought, we'd all thought, the boat had been destroyed as well. I couldn't ask now, not with that expression on Elizabeth's face. Instead, I prompted, "Lissa discovered the fire?"

"It had started in a cabinet underneath the built-in burners. We're still in the process of converting a home kitchen to a restaurant one," she added parenthetically. "When Lissa walked in, the flames had just leaped up and caught the curtains. Fortunately Lissa kept her head. She not only yelled, she turned the sink's hose attachment on the curtains, and then yanked them down. Kevin and I, and a friend, arrived at the same time. My friend ran downstairs and turned off the master fuses while Kevin phoned the fire department and I threw a pile of brand new tablecloths on the cupboard fire. You'll be able to see the rest of the story for yourself. Welcome to Rockcove Hall, Cindy. I'm sorry you had to arrive to this."

I scarcely heard the end, for she was turning right, between the scarlet and white flower borders of a wide drive. Ahead, on a slight rise, Rockcove Hall glowed in the sunset. Geraniums flaunted themselves in hanging baskets, and the fretwork railing of the widow's walk rose like a Spanish comb.

It was the house I had seen across the harbor, the enchanting mansion that had filled me with such a curious sense of déjà vu.

Elizabeth was already out of the car, pulling my luggage from the backseat. The screen door opened and a golden retriever hurled itself down the steps, followed by a sturdy blond boy who was the image of Dan Lancaster—eight-year-old Kevin— and a slight, dark-haired girl with bandaged arms.

I was swept inside, and my muddled sense of time was buried under the warmth of my welcome. Weariness engulfed me now that I had, at last, reached home port. A confused montage of images registered—the children hugging me; the cozy Victorian sitting room with the ell that was to become the guest registry and cashier's counter; the multiple, twisting flights of stairs; the lovely shock of the great, walnut-paneled drawing room with its paintings and crystal chandelier and Oriental rugs, its velvets and brocades.

The telephone was ringing, and Elizabeth ran for it. "You children show Cindy to her rooms," she called back. Kevin and the dog disappeared in the wake of an elderly workman who had shown up, so it was Lissa who reached for my suitcases with her bandaged hands.

"No, you don't!" I said sharply. She stopped, her odd gray-brown eyes hurt and remote. I hugged her quickly, but gingerly, because of the burns and bruises. "I'm not a guest, I'm family," I said firmly.

"And part of the hired help, to come right down to it. Now, how about my rooms? I want to change so I can help your mom get dinner."

"If we *can* get dinner," Lissa said somberly. "I'm not sure the stove works. And we can't use the lights in the kitchen yet." She led me back to the chintz-curtained sitting room, up two steps and down a corridor to another flight of narrow stairs. "Our rooms are up in this wing. Here's mine, and yours is next, and Kevin and Uncle Paul are across the hall. Mom and Daddy used to have the big one around the corner, above the Walnut Room. But Mom said since that's the best room, it should be used for the paying guests, so she's moved over to the east wing for the summer."

Lissa opened a door, and I stood on the threshold, enchanted.

The room was not large, but it had a fireplace. It was a private sitting room, with a velvet love seat and chintz-covered curve-backed Victorian easy chairs. A matching rose floral print covered the walls and ceiling and draped the window above lace curtains that billowed in the breeze. The tiny bedroom lay behind and one step up, all pink and pale green, with a crocheted bedspread and a patchwork quilt folded at the foot of the bed.

"It is nice, isn't it?" Lissa read my mind. "Mine is, too, but I don't have a sitting room. Mom says I have to wait till I'm fourteen. She hopes we'll be able to rent out all the rooms, but so far we have reservations for only about a quarter. I wish we didn't have to have paying guests at all." She twisted around, doing an abrupt mood swing again. "I'm glad you're here though. I wish there were a door between our rooms, but the walls in this house are too thick. Uncle Paul and Kevin have a door between their rooms."

Lissa and I were already picking up again on the instinctive affection we'd felt before, years ago. "I was sort of surprised about the paying guests myself," I admitted. "I thought maybe you'd be moving back to Boston, after—" I hesitated.

"You can say it," Lissa said steadily. "After my dad was killed. Daddy wanted us to live at Rockcove Hall. He always expected us to someday." Her face flushed. "And that's the truth, even if Uncle Paul won't believe it."

"Why won't Paul believe it?" I asked, fascinated.

"Because he's still sore at Daddy for marrying Mom," she said scornfully. "Uncle Paul wanted Dad to stay in Rockport and work with boats and fishing, like all the other Lancasters have done. That's what Grandpa wanted too. Or at least for Daddy to come back here after law school. Only Daddy stayed in Boston, and Uncle Paul blamed Mom for that. And then after Grandpa died, Daddy was Uncle Paul's guardian, and Daddy was making him leave the cape and go to college." Lissa stopped. "Sometimes I think Uncle Paul's glad Daddy's accident gave him a good excuse not to go back to college."

"You don't mean that."

Lissa just gave me a long, curiously adult look.

"Your mother said something about Paul starting a charter service with his boat." She didn't answer. I tried again. "I'm surprised your mother didn't open an art gallery instead of an inn. Or go back to art if she wanted to work . . . But I suppose sometimes, if someone close to you dies, it's easier to try a whole different kind of life."

Except how different could it be, here on Dan's home turf? On Lancaster turf? The voice was back in my head again.

"That's not why Mom's starting the inn. It's because she says we need money and art doesn't pay enough. It's not Uncle Paul's boat, it's my father's. And my father didn't die. He was killed," Lissa said, carefully precise. Suddenly she leaned toward me, her eyes anguished.

"*Why*, Cindy? He was a very, very good sailor. How could he have an accident? And he would never, never let anyone go out in a storm. That's what Grandpa had taught him, and he taught us. So why did he go out in the storm that night? And if it was such an awful accident, why could the boat still be salvaged?"

"Lissa!" Elizabeth called. "Let Cindy get on with her unpacking, and you come down here."

Lissa went reluctantly, leaving me with a lot to think about: the sense of déjà vu I'd had on seeing the inn. And the sense I had had even earlier— reading Elizabeth's letter, talking to her on the phone—that something was gravely wrong. And Lissa's questions— why *had* someone with Dan's seagoing experience been killed? And, oh, yes, that fire. Hadn't something been said about other small setbacks and annoyances at Rockcove Hall? Suddenly, vivid in my mind, were the reactions of the supermarket clerk and Mrs. Castell when I'd said I was coming here. I tried to shrug the thoughts off as I unpacked as figments of my fertile imagination. Of Lissa's childish imagination. But Lissa, speaking to me just now, had not looked or sounded like a child.

Faintly, through my muddled fog of thought, I

heard a car engine, then laughter and voices, beneath my window. Then Elizabeth's voice, speaking gaily. "Cindy, how soon can you come down? We still have no electricity in the dining room or kitchen, but some friends have come to our rescue with Chinese food. And Paul is back."

I washed and changed clothes quickly. Elizabeth's voice had come not from the Victorian parlor, but farther off, to the left. So when I emerged into the corridor, I followed the sounds of talking around the bend, past the room Lissa said had been her parents', and into a square formal foyer from which the grand staircase swept down to the Walnut Room. It was dusk now, and the upper hall was dark, but lamplight glowed below. Elizabeth stood smiling at the foot, and as I started down, she turned to pluck the sleeve of a young man behind her.

"It's time you two should meet. My cousin and my brother-in-law!"

The young man turned, and I stopped transfixed. The figure in white shirt and immaculate chinos, glowering at me after a second's shock from under thick hair that gleamed gold in the lamplight was my companion from the train and bus.

Three

The others didn't notice. A tall blond woman came into the hall and called to Paul, who moved away. Then Kevin was there, and a pleasant man with brown crisply curling hair. Elizabeth came to lead me down, her arm around my waist. "Cindy, this is Ailsa Craig, the sculptor. Also a distant relative of Dan's, Lissa's godmother, my college roommate, and my dearest friend. And Steve McGovern, another old friend and our family lawyer. My cousin, Cindy Clayborne, who's come to save my life and sanity!"

Was I imagining things, or did Paul's shoulders, so ostentatiously turned on me, become alert? The moment passed. Ailsa shook hands, smiling. Steve McGovern gave me an appraising look. "Too bad you weren't here when the fun broke out this afternoon."

"I will be next time," I said evenly. Then I did a double-take at my own words.

He shot me a keen glance. "You think there will be a next time?"

"I mean the next time a crisis crops up, that's all."

"Oh, it will crop up," Ailsa Craig agreed ruefully. "Elizabeth, I wish you'd listen to the people who care about you before you get in too deep. The hotel business isn't easy. You're not a native, and you have no experience."

Elizabeth stood very still, but she seemed to grow taller, and her gold wedding band winked on her clenching fist. "Listen to me, all of you. I am not going to join you in the gallery, Ailsa, sweet as it is of you to ask me. I am not going to vanish back to Boston, Paul. Neither am I going into the day-tripper tourist business, like the carnival holding forth these days down on Bearskin Neck! You natives can disparage the tourists all you want, but I notice a good many of you don't mind dirtying your hands with tourist money!"

Both Steve and Ailsa had involuntary reactions, swiftly veiled. I remembered that McGovern was a banker here as well as a lawyer, and that Ailsa owned a gallery that presumably sold to the tourist trade.

"I'm opening a country inn, which is a very different proposition from a tourist trap. And as for native and nonnative—" Elizabeth drew a deep breath. "Rockcove Hall is Lancaster property right back to a colonial land grant. My husband was a Lancaster, my children are Lancasters, and Lancasters don't give up easily. Or scare easily. And neither does my family. Right, Cindy?"

"Right," I said staunchly.

"So you can just put that on the natives' grapevine!"

Kevin banged a gong. We moved into the dining

room, which was gray-blue and white and paneled
and lit with candles. I found Paul behind me.

"Why didn't you tell me who you were?" he
demanded.

"When did you give me a chance?" I countered.
"For that matter, why didn't you tell me *your*
name?"

He stalked away to the other side of the table.

It was an odd, interesting dinner, with light talk
and laughter on the surface and serious currents
underneath. Paul had been in Maine, seeing some
shipyard about repairs on Dan's boat, the *Sea
Witch*. He hadn't been expected back for two
more days. It had been Steve McGovern who'd
arrived, bringing some papers for Elizabeth to
sign, just as Lissa discovered the fire. Ailsa Craig
hadn't heard till hours later, when the local grapevine served up the news. Both were horrified.
There were hints, quickly slurred over at Elizabeth's
frown, of earlier disasters at the inn.

And through it all, the spell of Rockcove Hall
worked magic on me. It had Elizabeth's own tranquility: a peace in spite of, not in the absence of,
disturbance. We ate take-out Chinese food from
old Rockingham plates, and drank iced tea from
Sandwich glass. Even the cavernous kitchen, despite a gaping hole in the cabinets and soot and
dirty water left by firemen, was magical in the
light of kerosene lamps.

"We've always kept the lamps on hand for use
during storms," Elizabeth said, seeing me look at
them as we cleared up after dinner.

"Like when my father was killed." Lissa dropped
the words into the silence like glittering chips of
ice.

I saw Steve and Ailsa exchange glances. "Elizabeth, don't you think—" Ailsa started, and at the same time, Elizabeth said, "Kevin, it's past your bedtime."

Kevin's chin was thrust out stubbornly, and Lissa's lips were pressed close together. "I'll go up with them," I said, rising quickly. "I'm pretty tired myself. You all probably have a lot to talk about."

It was some time before I got to bed. First Kevin and Lissa had to show me their rooms. Kevin's showed divided loyalties. Sports-star posters decked the walls, but his furniture was sea-captain style. A watercolor by Elizabeth of the *Sea Witch* hung on the wall.

Lissa's room, with its canopied bed, was as fragile and orderly as she was herself. Her lace-draped windows, like mine, looked out toward the sea; Kevin's had faced the road.

"Uncle Paul's got the corner room. He can see both ways," Kevin boasted. "He's going to give me the first ride when the *Sea Witch* is fixed. Do you like boats, Cindy?"

"*Shut up!*" Lissa burst out tightly. I gave Kevin a ferocious frown and pointed him toward the shower, then I followed Lissa into her room and closed the door. Lissa was standing, staring out the window toward the point of rocks.

"Kevin doesn't understand," she said. "Not really. Oh, he misses Daddy a lot, but he was only seven. Beside, he wasn't awake that night. He didn't see."

"See what?" I asked gently.

Lissa shook her head. "I don't want to talk about it. Stay here while I take my shower, okay?" She went into our shared bathroom, shutting the door behind her primly. I sat down in the Windsor rocker, and after a while the door opened slightly and Deborah, the golden retriever, wandered in to offer a sociable paw. Presently Lissa came back, looking younger and more vulnerable in her pale blue nightgown. I half-expected her to pick up our earlier conversation, but she did not. She got into bed, and the dog jumped up beside her. I reached for the bureau lamp.

"You can't put that out," Kevin said from the doorway.

He planted himself, legs apart, arms folded, and regarded his sister mockingly. "Lissa's too much of a baby to sleep in the dark. She sees things."

"*Kevin!*"

"Okay, you have nightmares," Kevin corrected himself amiably. "Anyway," he went on to me, "we have to leave the light on or she screams."

Lissa sat up in fury. "Kevin Lancaster, you remember when you sneaked down to watch that late-night movie on TV Mom said we shouldn't see? Remember how you ran in here, and what you told me?"

Two pairs of Lancaster eyes locked in silent battle. Abruptly Kevin turned tail and left. "You'd better take Deborah out with you," Lissa murmured, settling beneath the covers. "Mom says we mustn't let her get in the habit, or she'll think she has the right to sleep with guests."

I went back to my room—or suite, actually—with a lot to think about. The old rooms enfolded me. When I had undressed, I stood before the bureau's heavy mirror brushing out my hair and had the oddest sensation that I had stepped back through time a hundred years or more. My white

cotton nightgown, with its eyelet frills, had, like
these rooms, the look of an earlier time. Through
the window I heard Steve McGovern's car pull
away, and Elizabeth calling a warm good-bye. Floors
creaked as she walked back toward the kitchen.

Unaccountably the electric lights in my bedroom dimmed. The reflection in the mirror shimmered, seemed to change. I was looking at myself,
yet not myself. The dark plastic brush in my hand,
reflected, showed a glint of silver; my eyes, a glint
of gold. And I looked older. The phenomenon
lasted only a moment, during which I was caught
as motionless as a creature trapped in amber. Then
the lamps brightened again, and I told myself
what I knew was true: Electricity everywhere
could suffer momentary "brownouts" during peri-
ods of heavy use, and in any event, today's electrical fire had undoubtedly caused damage to the
wiring.

No one else seemed to have noticed. There
were no sounds from the children, and Elizabeth's
footsteps still moved downstairs as tranquilly as
before. Even Deborah, who had followed me into
my rooms and was now draped decoratively across
the bedroom rug, was untroubled.

I had turned out all lamps except the one on the
bedside table, when Elizabeth knocked softly and
asked if I was awake.

"Come on in," I called.

Elizabeth had undressed. In her flounced wrap-
per, with her hair down, she looked girlish, all
except her eyes. "I just wanted to be sure you
have everything you need to feel at home," she
said, smiling.

I laughed. "If you make all your guests feel this

welcome, Rockcove Hall is going to do a booming
business!"

"That's what I'm counting on you to help with! I
want this to be like the country-house hotels Dan
and I visited in England." Elizabeth sat on the bed
by Deborah and scratched her ears. "Cindy, I am
glad you could come. It's good to have someone
around me I can trust."

"You have Steve McGovern, and your friend
Ailsa," I said, startled. "And you said you had very
dependable help coming from the village."

"Yes, of course. But you're family. That makes a
difference." After a moment Elizabeth's smile flashed.
"I have to confess, I had an ulterior motive in
asking you. Rockport is Lancaster country. I'm the
outlander who lured Dan away from his rightful
place. If I stay here fifty years, I'll *still* be an
outlander."

"But you're staying."

"Of course. Kevin and Lissa are Lancasters; I
don't want them to be outlanders. Besides, we
love it here. Dan loved it. We always expected to
spend our summers here once Dan was a partner
in his law firm and didn't have to be on twenty-
four-hour call." Her eyes twinkled. "He could
commute from Boston—you've already experienced
that—and I could paint here. When he made
partnership and inherited the hall from his grandfather two years ago, we decided to make it a
year-round move. Of course, that trestle rail bridge
hadn't been burned out then. Dan could make the
trip in an hour." She fell silent.

"And then afterward . . . you decided to stay on
anyway," I prompted.

"I never considered anything else. We'd sold

the Waltham house, and the children could feel closer to Dan here. I want that for them. Besides," Elizabeth went on, deliberately matter-of-fact, "I have to do something. There turned out not to be as much money as I'd expected, and using the hall seemed the most practical thing to do. Dan and his grandfather would have approved. Actually Dan and I had discussed the inn idea as a retirement-days possibility. The time for it just came sooner than expected. . . . My other ulterior motive for having you here was the children. You'll be good for them, Lissa especially. She's having a great deal of difficulty accepting Dan's accident."

"She seems to . . . have trouble accepting it *as* an accident," I ventured.

"The accident was because of the storm. Dan was too good a seaman for it to have happened otherwise." Elizabeth's voice grew hard. "And too good a lawyer. Someone needed him. An emergency. He told me to go back to sleep and he'd see me in the morning."

I knew what had happened next. In the morning the *Sea Witch* had been found on the rocks beyond the point, and Dan had been missing. Washed overboard, apparently—in spite of the fact that he'd taken the cruiser, rather than a dinghy, because the large boat had seemed safer. Two days later his body had been found.

Elizabeth straightened. "So! If this is confession time, what were *your* reasons for helping out this decrepit relative? An urgent desire not to visit museums with your father? I've heard about those excursions more than once from your mother," she added as I blushed.

"That's not all," I confessed. "Somebody I've

been dating has a summer job on a newspaper in Gloucester before he starts college."

"Hmm. You should have an interesting summer," Elizabeth said. I was glad to see amusement flicker in her eyes. "I was planning to make a round of the papers tomorrow, placing ads. Perhaps you'd like to tend to that errand for me. Sleep well, honey." She left, turning out the light for me as she did so, and Deborah went with her.

The old house settled slowly for the night, like a teakettle slowly subsiding from the boil. A faint sea breeze stirred the curtains, and the scent of flowers drifted from the seaside gardens.

I don't know if I waked or slept, but presently I was vaguely conscious of gazing at the bureau mirror. I knew I was looking at it from my pillows, not from before the mirror. I thought I was seeing again that form of a young woman reflected on the clouded glass, a young woman with long chestnut hair in a long white nightgown. And moments later—*was* it moments, or was sleep playing tricks on me?—I heard a sound of weeping.

I sat up, blinking, but only the curtains were reflected now. That, and faint moonlight. The despairing, muffled sound of long-drawn-out sobbing lingered.

Lissa, I thought. But when I tiptoed through the bathroom to her bedroom, she was fast asleep, the night-light burning dimly. And when I crept back to my own room, the sound had ceased.

Four

The sunlight woke me when it was barely six A.M. I threw the window wide and leaned out, drinking in the sights and scents. Sea gulls wheeled in a brilliant sky, and the smell of salt mingled with the sweetness of June roses. Elizabeth, in a sundress, walked along the rocks at the sea edge with Deborah running in circles around her. Last night's visions seemed very far away.

I pulled on jeans and a big shirt and went downstairs as Elizabeth came in, her arms full of flowers. "I'm trying to train myself to a daily routine before the guests start arriving," she said, laughing. "Operating under the delusion I can make things easy! Come on out to the kitchen and I'll give you coffee. You want breakfast now or later?"

"Wait a minute. I'm hired help, not a paying guest."

"In that case *you* can arrange the flowers. The vases are on shelves in the butler's pantry." She led the way through the kitchen into an airy room, where glass-doored cabinets, ceiling-high, rose above a multitude of drawers and cupboards. There was a stainless-steel sink here, too, and another refrigerator, and an electric coffeepot. I took down vases as Elizabeth poured coffee into mugs.

"The carpenters will be here at ten to start work on the kitchen. Since I have to have them, I decided to splurge on the rest of the changes I'd been putting off. A stainless-steel restaurant range, refrigerator, and freezer. And a warming oven. As Steve keeps pointing out, this 'innkeeping brainstorm' needs a sizable cash investment if it's going to succeed." She sighed.

"And he doesn't think you should do it?"

"He thinks I'm being sentimental and impractical, given the circumstances. 'If Dan were still here with a lawyer's income coming in, it would be one thing, but for a woman with dependent children and no business background to saddle herself with this old monstrosity,' et cetera. Some monstrosity; the hall's a Bulfinch landmark!"

"Bulfinch?"

"A famous architect from the clipper ship era. He designed the Massachusetts State House, among other things. The hall's mentioned in a lot of books about historic architecture. Steve agrees with Ailsa that the offers to buy I've had are too lucrative to turn down."

"And leave Cape Ann?"

Elizabeth, to my surprise, colored slightly. "Not necessarily," she said briefly. All at once the way Steven McGovern had looked at her a few times started making sense. She rose. "Come on, let's take our coffee out on the terrace, and then I'll give you the grand tour while we're still free of distractions."

We went out the kitchen door and down wind-
ing flower-edged steps cut in the slope. The slate
terrace ran along the hall's harbor side at what
might be called basement level. Actually the door
Elizabeth opened off the terrace led into a com-
fortable, sprawling TV room. "No television in the
guest rooms—yet. We'll tell them it's to preserve
the eighteenth-century tranquility." Elizabeth smiled
at me. "During the summer, buffet lunch will be
available on the terrace and in the grape arbor.
Our cook and waitress from the village will take
care of that."

Half the terrace was roofed over by the extension jutting out from the floor above. "Formerly
our screened porch, now our guest dining room,"
Elizabeth said, pointing upward. "Fortunately there
are glass panels we can pull shut at the demands of
weather. You and I will take turns hostessing, and
four times a week you'll wait tables."

Beyond the garden steps, almost buried in the
sloping lawn, rose a shallow pointed roof crowned
with a weather vane. "What's that?" I asked,
nodding toward it.

"The carriage house. It's off limits. Too much
rusting junk inside that could hurt the children.
Come see the swimming pool!"

We crossed the lawn to the pool terrace, with its
turquoise umbrella tables and chairs and lounges
inside a snow-white fence. More turquoise-cushioned
chairs and swings dotted the lawns. Back inside,
we made the downstairs circuit, with Deborah as
an eager attendant at our heels. Elizabeth showed
me through the two floors of bedrooms, all
charmingly nostalgic and furnished with antiques.

"They're Lancaster family pieces, which I will

not sell. There are ten double rooms available for renting, which means twenty guests. Plus we could put in an additional ten cots for children." I could see she was doing arithmetic in her head.

"It's none of my business," I said impulsively, "but are you having real money problems? Lissa said . . . I mean, I don't really *have* to have a salary, and I'm sure my father . . ."

"Absolutely not," Elizabeth said promptly. "It's sweet of you to offer, but this inn's going to operate on a businesslike basis or not at all."

We were now on the third floor, which occupied only the main central block of Rockcove Hall, standing in the central hall. Sunlight poured in through the tall Palladian window in the stairwell. There were four large rooms up here, each with its own small inner room and bath. A locked door led to the attic where, Elizabeth said, other antiques and collectibles and just plain junk were stored. "Lancasters have lived here for two hundred years, so you can imagine how much has accumulated. The children love to play up there on rainy days."

There was another unlabeled door in the hall, shut with a new and extremely businesslike dead bolt. "Where does that go?" I asked.

"To the widow's walk. I can't have the children, or inn guests, going there. The railings are so old, they could be unsafe." Elizabeth sat down on a carved cedar chest, her face still grave. "We were talking about finances. I think I had better tell you how things stand in case you find yourself answering strange telephone calls. I have Dan's insurance money, which will come in installments over the next ten years. That's earmarked for the children's education. And I get social security payments for them; that will last till they're nineteen, in college. Other than that—" She hesitated. "Dan and I were putting our savings, and the money we made on the sale of the Waltham house, into investments. Mostly as what's called venture capital. That meant Dan put money into other people's new businesses—like this inn. You can make, or lose, a good deal of money that way. But Dan had a good head on his shoulders and I trusted him. Only—"

"Only?" I prompted.

Elizabeth spread her hands. "Only it seems some of the people he invested with weren't so trustworthy. Or we'd hit a bad economic climate, or something. When Dan's estate was settled, it turned out most of his current investments were practically worthless."

"Oh."

Elizabeth grinned. "So if anybody phones trying to sell us a boatyard, or shipping rights, or oil rights, hang up. Actually you're more apt to answer calls from real estate companies trying to buy the hall. Or impressive-sounding firms wanting to take those worthless securities off my hands. Being a suspicious-minded New Englander, I'm not selling."

"You mean those investments might be worth something after all?"

Elizabeth shrugged. "Maybe on a snowy day in August, fifty years from now. All I know is, nobody's offering something for nothing, and as a general rule people offer less, not more, than what they want is worth. So until I know what's behind those phone calls, I'm 'not sellin' nuthin',' as our handyman would say." She glanced at her watch.

"Come on, we'd better get the kids fed before the carpenters arrive."

Lissa and Kevin were in the kitchen eating cereal and doughnuts at the scrubbed pine table. "We thought you'd left for town already," Lissa said. "The car's gone."

Elizabeth frowned. "Paul must have taken it! I hope he brings it back soon. Cindy and I have errands to do in Gloucester."

"You could get Steve to take you," Kevin offered.

"No, they couldn't. Don't be silly!" Lissa said sharply.

"Could so. *You're* the one that's silly," Kevin said stubbornly. Lissa's face went pale, then darkened.

"Elizabeth, I almost forgot to ask," I said hastily. "There aren't any paying guests here yet, I know. Are any others of the inn staff staying here? You didn't show me any employees' rooms when we made the tour."

"There aren't any employees' rooms," Elizabeth said. "Except ours, I suppose. Why?"

"It's funny. I could have sworn I—well, that I heard someone else in the inn last night. A woman."

"Crying." The way Lissa said it, it was a statement, not a question. I stared at her.

"That's the way it sounded. I peeked in at you, but you were sleeping. It sounded as if it was coming from next door to me, or above me."

"It was the wind," Kevin said promptly. There was something in his tone that was odd, and I swung around to him.

"You know it wasn't," Lissa said so softly I wasn't sure she'd even spoken. She had stopped eating and was staring at her place. "It's the Watcher."

At least that's what I thought she said. Afterward I wasn't sure, the moment had passed so quickly. Elizabeth said briskly, as if she hadn't heard, "Kevin's right. The wind can play strange tricks in these old houses. . . . Oh, good, there's Paul."

She was looking out the window with evident relief.

Five

I had no chance to ask Elizabeth, or Lissa either, about the Watcher. Paul came in and sat down to eat, and Elizabeth immediately began laying out the day's schedule, including our trip to Gloucester.

"Don't you have to be here for the workmen?" I asked. She shook her head.

"Ailsa's being an angel and coming to supervise. She's good at design, and we've planned the kitchen remodeling together. Even if she doesn't approve of what I'm up to," Elizabeth finished gaily. "Ailsa's sculpture work is structural; she's had to learn so much about metalwork and carpentry and engineering in the course of it that she's as good as any contractor. And Paul promised he'd stay around all day too."

So shortly after ten Elizabeth and I set out in the car for Gloucester. She would drop me at the newspaper office with copy for the ad and pen-and-ink sketches to be reproduced in a brochure. "Then while you're establishing cordial relations with the press, I'll go pick out my new refrigerator and some more dishes. If I'd ever known two months ago how much driving around's involved in opening a business! Do you have a driver's license, Cindy?"

I confessed to having a new one but not much road experience.

"Then you can take over the local errands as soon as I give you some training on this car and the Rockport roads. Don't worry, I won't send you out on the highway or down through Depot Square! We'll avoid the center of town today anyway. It's a gorgeous day and the tourists will be out in droves."

The ride to Gloucester seemed much shorter than my trip out from there on the bus had been. Before I knew it, Elizabeth was pulling up in front of the modern stone-and-glass newspaper building. "You look fine, stop worrying!" she scolded me lightly. "Besides, since the boy never had a chance to learn you were coming up here, he'll probably be bowled over by sheer surprise."

I hoped that it would be a welcome one. Bill Rhodes had fascinated me for longer than I wanted to admit, but he'd never particularly seemed to notice me until this spring. He was the star of the basketball team and had edited the school paper the past year. We'd shared a Spanish class all year long, but we'd never done much more than said hi—until he'd broken up with his girlfriend. Not long after I'd heard the news, he'd totally astonished me by leaning across the aisle in class and inviting me to the senior prom.

The prom, and the breakfast party and day at the shore that went along with it, had been sheer heaven. It could have been the start of something . . . except that Bill was leaving for his summer job the very next day, and going straight from that to college, whereas I hadn't known yet whether my Rockport summer was going to materialize or not, and felt shy about mentioning the possibility.

But now I was on Cape Ann, and so was he, and I had a perfectly valid reason for seeing him that could not seem pushy. I went into the newspaper lobby, and there he was, standing with his back to me as he hunted through a file drawer. I would have known those broad shoulders and that shining dark hair anywhere. A buzzer had gone off as I entered. "Be with you in one moment," he said absently, without turning.

"That's all right," I said, just as businesslike. And then he did swing around. His reaction was all that I desired.

"*Cindy?* Wow, what are you doing here? Hey, you look great!" In the two weeks since he'd graduated and come up here, his tan had darkened to near mahogany. His blue eyes were very bright against the tan, and they showed that he was genuinely pleased to see me.

"I'm working up here," I said demurely. "General assistant, out at Rockcove Hall."

"That's the old sea captain's place that's opening as an inn, isn't it? How'd *you* land there?"

"Family connections," I said airily. "It's all sort of happened since you've been away. I'm here to place an ad."

Bill got down to business then, calling in the advertising manager and then the woman who handled the job printing. "How about lunch?" he asked when we were finished.

"I wish I could. But Elizabeth—that's my cousin— will be back any minute. We have a lot of work to do. The inn has to be ready for opening next week, and yesterday there was a fire." I stopped abruptly, not knowing whether Elizabeth wanted that talked about or not.

"There's a story about that being written up right now. People are interested because of the boat accident last year." Bill's eyes narrowed. "Is that your cousin? The wife of the man who was drowned? My uncle was telling me about that last week."

"That's not the kind of publicity the inn needs."

His face softened. "Don't worry, my uncle won't sensationalize the fire. I can see you're going to be busy all this week, but you'll be able to get some free time once the place opens, won't you?"

I laughed. "If it's as successful as Elizabeth hopes, none of us will have time for anything but work!"

"Then I'll just have to kidnap you," he threatened. I went out into the noontime heat with my heart singing.

The rest of that day went quickly. Back at Rockcove Hall workmen were in possession. Elizabeth and I and the children moved onto the back lawn, spray-painting second-hand restaurant tables and chairs. The sun was hot, and I could feel my shoulders burning, but we stopped only for a brief dip in the pool in the early afternoon. Ailsa Craig joined us. Elizabeth protested that she was too busy to swim. She was running here and there, tending to a dozen things at once. When the electrician came out for the third time to report that he was having trouble getting wiring through the hall's solid walls, Ailsa intervened.

"For heaven's sake, Elizabeth, knock off and let me tend to it! I know these buildings better than you do; I practically grew up here. Now, get in the pool and I'll find another way of routing those expensive appliances of yours, since you're so determined to proceed with this foolhardy plan!"

Elizabeth wearily joined me in the pool.

"She's really against the inn idea, isn't she?" I asked when Ailsa was safely gone.

"Ailsa," Elizabeth said, "still wants to see me the way we saw ourselves in art school—dedicated artists in ivory-tower garrets, far above the crass concerns of commerce." She giggled, seeming all at once that girl again. "Of course, she's blithely overlooking the fact that she's being pretty crass herself, wanting me to sell Rockcove Hall for real estate development. Even if that would mean I could spend the rest of my life painting exquisite paintings for love, not money, I'd never do it. Ailsa knows that. She'd understand it if she weren't so determined to be my mother hen!"

"Where does Steve McGovern come in?" I asked daringly.

Elizabeth didn't answer. "How was your rendez-vous with your newspaper hero?" she inquired pointedly.

"Fine. He was pleasantly surprised to see me." If she could use offense as a defense, so could I. "Maybe while the electricians are here you should have them check the brownout."

"They have. Twice. There's no explanation they can find, so it has to be from a power cutback." Elizabeth broke off. "Who's that gorgeous creature?"

I looked up toward the road, and all at once my heart was behaving erratically. "That's Bill Rhodes," I murmured, feeling my face turn pink.

He was striding down the steps from the driveway, a broad grin on his face and a large basket on each arm. "If you're too busy to go out, I figured you could use some help. I'm a fair carpenter and a good painter, and I've brought my own supper. Mrs. Lancaster? I'm Bill Rhodes." He reached out a firm arm to shake hands.

The baskets contained lobsters enough for all. By the time Paul came from the house, looking tired and dirty, and Steve McGovern arrived, Bill and Kevin were hitting it off famously and were starting to set up a cookout.

"That's not the way I told you to do that, Kevin." Paul was at his most belligerent, ignoring Bill completely.

"Paul's our resident lobsterman," Elizabeth said easily, performing introductions. Behind the boys' backs her eyes met mine, full of mischief. Then Steve and Ailsa entered the conversation to lighten it, and I showed Kevin and Lissa how to spread ears of corn with butter, onion salt and cayenne pepper the way my father did, then roll them up in foil for roasting, and the tension eased.

Or it seemed to. Like last night the dinner scene and conversation were idyllic. But underneath something stirred and seethed like the fog beginning to roll in across the harbor.

It wasn't till we were having coffee around the fireplace in the TV room that the "something" began to take on nebulous form. The electric lights flickered and then went out completely, and Paul groaned. "Elizabeth, we're going to have to have this place totally rewired."

"It's out of the question," Steve said firmly. He stopped as Elizabeth glanced warningly toward

Bill. Rockcove's financial affairs were not to be discussed before a stranger.

"Anyway, it's very romantic," Elizabeth said, lighting kerosene lamps to supplement the firelight. "That's the promotional angle we'll take with our guests."

"Speaking of guests and promotion"—Bill cleared his throat—"my uncle's paper would like to run a piece about the opening." He held up a notebook sheepishly. "I've been taking notes. We'll send a photographer out to get a proper picture in the daytime, but would you mind if I try one now of the point in the fog? I have a time exposure and a flash."

For an instant everything seemed to stop, and with sharp clarity I felt as if I were seeing into Elizabeth's mind. Seeing the fog and storm a year ago, and newspaper pictures of its aftermath...Steve McGovern moved closer to Elizabeth, protectively, and Ailsa put up a hand as if warding off danger.

I knew Bill was suddenly remembering the accident too. He reddened. "I don't mean any personal story on the place," he said hastily. "Just about its historic significance—and the antiques. They ought to be surefire customer draws. And didn't I hear something said at the paper about a ghost?"

I found my heart was pounding. Then Elizabeth laughed.

"You mean that old chestnut about the captain's lady? For goodness' sake, don't dredge that up again!"

All at once the balloon of silence was burst. "Stop hiding your head in the sand," Steve said roughly, and Ailsa went over and lifted Elizabeth's face to hers.

"It has been dredged up, and you know it, Beth. It has been ever since Dan died. The Watcher walks, and a Lancaster dies. The story's been floating around again ever since that old coot Asey Dawson started insisting he'd seen the Watcher the night of Dan's accident. He was trying to blame the accident that night on fright, not drink, and everybody knows it. But you're a fool if you think the story isn't going to reach your paying guests!"

"Maybe," Elizabeth said shakily, "they'll consider it a drawing card. All the same," she added, eyeing Bill, "it's not the sort of publicity I want."

"I won't print a word of this," Bill said quickly. "I swear by my union card! My uncle wouldn't let me anyway. Not unless there were some evidence." He held up his camera, trying to lighten the conversation with some humor. "Maybe I could get an astral photograph of—what did you call her anyway? The captain's lady?"

"She's the Watcher," Lissa said tightly, "and it isn't funny." All at once she was on her feet, shaking convulsively. Paul reached out a hand toward her, and she shrank away. "No! You're always telling me it's silly, but it isn't. And you know it. You're nothing but liars, all of you!"

She ran for the stairs, and I went after her.

I found her halfway up the stairs to our rooms, bent over double, sobbing. I went toward her hesitantly, and then something held me back. Someone else was in the hallway with us. I did not know who it could be, but I was not afraid. And then all of a sudden the electricity went on, and

Lissa and I were alone—except for Elizabeth, coming up the stairs.

"I'll put the children to bed," Elizabeth said quietly. "You go back to your guest."

So I went back down to the TV room, and sent Kevin up, and soon after that Bill left with his fog photograph untaken. Steve went, and Ailsa and Paul and I made the rounds of the hall together to close it for the night.

Paul said little as we did so. But when we were up in the corridor between his room and mine, he gave me another of those appraising glares.

"You mustn't encourage Lissa with this Watcher business. It's all garbage."

"I wasn't planning to encourage her," I said. "But a little respect and sympathy might be good for her."

"Not if it makes her more keyed up," he said curtly. "The kid's having a hard enough time as it is. Especially with McGovern trying to make a move on Elizabeth."

I had no answer, so I said nothing. And that was that, except when I went into my rooms, I found a small iridescent glass sphere on my pillow. One of Lissa's treasures, I thought tenderly. She must have felt my concern, though it was unexpressed.

I put the sphere on my bureau and went to bed. And that night I felt no sense of a watching presence, not even in my dreams.

Six

When I awoke Sunday morning, the uneasiness of
the night before seemed very far away. The glass
sphere rested quietly on the lace runner, iridescent and faintly pink. *I won't say anything about it
to Lissa till we're alone,* I thought. She had given
it to me in secret; I would thank her in secret too.
The bond between us, so immediate and so unde-
niable, was strengthening.

The bond between myself and Elizabeth too.... I
wouldn't think about what was happening between
myself and Bill, I told myself as I ran downstairs to
breakfast.

What about Paul? The words came out of nowhere, so intensely I could have sworn someone
had spoken them aloud. No one had, yet the
impression brought me up short on the landing.

Instead of going straight to the kitchen, I stepped
outside through the sitting room door. A fresh
breeze brought salt and the scent of flowers to me,
and sunlight sparkled on the surface of the sea.
And there he was, Paul, a small figure with his
back to me, bent over a small dory down by the

point of rocks. I turned away and stood for several seconds, breathing deeply, before I went inside.

I had no chance to speak privately with Lissa all that day. Elizabeth had that party to cater—not on the Rockcove Hall premises, thank goodness. We drove to Ailsa's, and while she took the children and me to church, Elizabeth took over the kitchen with Paul's surprising help. After church, followed by lemonade and cookies on the church lawn, Ailsa took the three of us to the Blacksmith House restaurant for lunch. "Elizabeth wouldn't appreciate having to stop working long enough for a civilized meal," she said ruefully.

I looked at her. "Miss Craig—"

"Call me Ailsa. Everyone does. Besides, we're distant in-laws, aren't we?" Ailsa's eyes twinkled. "Dan and I were second cousins once removed."

"Ailsa." I smiled back, but I was serious. "You're opposed to this inn idea, aren't you?"

We could speak freely, for Kevin and Lissa were over at the windows, watching sea gulls wheeling in the harbor. "Not opposed," Ailsa said, searching for words. "More—concerned. Elizabeth doesn't have business experience, and trying to make money in a resort community can be wicked. She's such a good artist, I hate to see her not have time for that. And she—frankly, she's throwing over an iron-clad opportunity for very good money in favor of a quixotic plan that could lose her everything. She can't be sure Rockcove Hall will work out as a hotel. She's charging high prices, and then there are all those stories—"

The waitress appeared with our food, and the children returned, and we had to drop the subject.

I had no chance to resume the conversation

later either. Back at Ailsa's sprawling house, a combination home-gallery-studio, we were all put to work. Kevin made salad; Lissa helped Paul and Elizabeth cook. It was as if, removed from Rockcove Hall, we were transformed into an efficiently working machine. At five o'clock a pleasant matronly woman and an angular younger one arrived, both in white uniforms. Elizabeth changed into simple dark linen, and they drove the baskets of food over to the client's house. Paul and I cleaned up Ailsa's kitchen, companionable for once. Then he drove the children and me back to the hall.

During that ride his mood changed. He scarcely spoke, and as soon as we were out of the car, he drove away, while I was still trying to unlock the front door.

The hall was all in darkness. But it did not feel threatening. I noticed that; I remembered it afterward. The darkness was warm and velvety and enfolding. I lit a lamp, and Deborah came to greet us, pushing her silky muzzle into our hands. There was again that sense of presence, but it was welcoming.

"I'm not used to old houses. This is just that sense of *aliveness* all old houses have," I thought. I foraged in the refrigerator for snacks, and invited the children to my room for a picnic and some games.

I hadn't gotten Ailsa to explain what she meant by stories about Rockcove Hall, and I hadn't thanked Lissa for the glass sphere. Actually I'd forgotten about it till I saw it glimmering in the faint moonlight that came through my bedroom window. Tomorrow, I promised myself, and fell asleep. And that night, again, I heard no weeping.

Monday was hot and sun-bright and brisk and hectic. When I came down in the morning, Elizabeth was sitting at the kitchen table holding her coffee cup in her left hand and with her right making rapid notes on several lists.

"The chamber of commerce called. They have several bookings for us for the Fourth of July weekend," she said, not looking up. I already knew the association acted as a general clearing house through which hotels and motels that were fully booked could refer requests for reservations to other lodgings. So Rockcove Hall was now officially in business, even if no direct calls had come in yet in response to the ads Elizabeth had placed in the New York and Boston papers.

Paul came in from outdoors in time to hear this. He looked around the kitchen with disfavor. "You better just hope all these repairs get done in time." His face was tight; he was the Paul of the bus again.

"They have to," Elizabeth said absently. She pushed her chair back and rubbed her eyes. "You're giving Asey a hand with the kitchen today, aren't you?"

"I'm meeting Pablo at the shipyard in an hour," Paul said flatly.

Elizabeth's face fell. "Oh, *Paul!* You promised."

"Look, do you want the *Sea Witch* available to cart your fancy guests around like you advertised, or not? I gave you all day yesterday. Today Pablo needs me to help install the *Witch's* new engine. If you weren't using the fire as an excuse to make your precious kitchen over, Asey could probably have gotten the damage repaired already!"

Paul's raw antagonism took my breath away. Not

Elizabeth's. I noticed that even then. She was not even startled. "It's not my kitchen—"

"You could have fooled me. But then, I just grew up here. You've lived here only a couple of years, but Rockcove Hall does belong to you now, doesn't it?"

Kevin wen' on eating his cereal stolidly. I could sense Lissa starting to shake.

"That's not what we're talking about. This is your home, too, for as long as you want, and you know it. But the kitchen belongs to a *hotel* now, and the remodeling is only practical."

"Then it's a good thing some firebug decided to play fun and games out here, isn't it?" Paul demanded.

"*Stop it,*" Lissa said very low.

I interrupted quickly, half in earnest, half to change the subject. "What firebug?"

"Excuse me, I forgot that as an outlander you aren't plugged into our quaint little gossip hotline," Paul said sarcastically. "The fire *has* to have been set. It could have been villagers who object to the hall being used as an inn. Or outraged competitors who don't want to share the wealth. Or those nebulous real estate operators who want to drive the Lancasters into selling. Or our family ghost; take your pick. I know the old girl's supposed to be a killer, but I never heard before now that she's a pyro."

"*Stop it!*" Lissa repeated, this time loudly. She ran out. Paul stopped, his face a mixture of realization and dismay that would have been funny at any other time.

"I think," Elizabeth said very quietly, "you'd better leave for Gloucester."

I cleared the dirty dishes off the table, and discussed the reservations with Elizabeth over toast and orange juice. And when the time seemed right, I went in search of Lissa.

I found her sitting on the point of rocks, pale in the sunlight, in her characteristic pose, arms locked around her knees. She was gazing off across the harbor and gave no acknowledgment of my approach. But I knew she was aware that I was there. I sat down, too, wordlessly. After several minutes Lissa spoke, not turning.

"He shouldn't have said that. About the Watcher being a killer and a—a firebug. It isn't true."

"Who is the Watcher?"

"I don't want to talk about it."

"Well, if you do feel like it anytime," I said, carefully casual, "I'd like to hear."

"You'd laugh at me too."

"No, I wouldn't." There was no response. "By the way," I said at last, gently, "thank you for giving me that glass sphere. You knew I was upset that night, didn't you? It was one of your special things, wasn't it?"

Lissa turned to look straight at me, her eyes opaque. "It isn't mine," she said gravely.

Then Elizabeth called us, and we went inside.

Seven

The days before the Fourth of July weekend passed quickly, like shifting patterns in a kaleidoscope. There were some constants—work, and swimming, and suppers on the porch or patio. Martha Gibbs and Ella Hazen, whom I'd met at Ailsa's house on Sunday, came several times. They were the cook and the waitress Elizabeth had hired. As a part-time waitress, I sat in on their briefing sessions. Elizabeth was brisk, businesslike, and firm about her wishes. The hall's atmosphere was not to be down-east folksy; it was to be a cross between New England aristocracy and English country house. Guests were to be treated with formal etiquette and a gracious reserve. Martha grew speechless and Ella sniffed, but I was impressed. Ailsa could stop worrying about Elizabeth, I thought.

Asey Dawson was at Rockcove Hall daily, doing carpentry or light plumbing or helping the electricians. He was a real New England jack-of-all-trades, his pipe perpetually clutched between his discolored teeth, his weathered rubbery face anywhere from sixty to, as Elizabeth said, "half as old as God." He was a fixture on the cape, a member by blood or his own assertion of all the old families—including the Lancasters—somewhere way back when. He, not the Coast Guard, had found Dan Lancaster's body washed up on the rocks.

"He must have been out looking before there was light in the sky," Elizabeth said. "I hadn't gotten to sleep till almost five, and then only because Ailsa insisted I take a sleeping pill. It was the night after the one when Dan went out and—didn't come back."

It was late afternoon, the day before the first guests were to arrive, and the two of us were taking a breather on the terrace. Elizabeth had started telling me the story as an explanation of why she was having difficulty standing up to Asey on the matter of how the kitchen cabinets should look. It was the first time anyone except Lissa had really talked about the accident to me. "Ailsa came here as soon as the storm was over and the Coast Guard found the *Sea Witch*, wrecked. And Steve came too. They stayed all that day and that night, even after the Coast Guard gave up searching for Dan's body. *Asey* didn't give up. I must have been deep, deep asleep, but all of a sudden I sat straight up in bed, as though something had called me."

She closed her eyes briefly. Then she went on, as though talking to someone who was both kin and a fellow outlander was a release. "I went up to the widow's walk, and there was Asey coming along the beach in the red dawn with Dan in his arms. He'd found him washed up against the rocks. The police were furious at him for moving the body, but Asey just said there was 'nuthin' nobody could've done, an' it warn't seemly to leave a Lancaster a-lyin' thar.'" She was silent, remembering.

"Ailsa said something about Asey being drunk," I suggested delicately. Elizabeth made an impatient gesture.

"Ailsa's furious because Asey went around all last summer insisting he'd seen the Watcher out on the point, and that a phantom boat loomed out of the fog right in front of him. You see, Asey ran his skiff into the *Sea Witch* that night, just as Dan was pulling away. Anyway, Asey claimed it happened because he had to swerve to avoid the 'ghost boat,' as he called her, and ran into the *Sea Witch* instead."

I stared at her. "You mean *Asey* caused Dan's accident?"

"Oh, no! Asey's little boat couldn't possibly have caused Dan's crash. But Asey felt just terrible about it all the same, and everybody knows Asey was undoubtedly plastered at the time. He hadn't done the *Sea Witch* any real harm, just gashed the paint. You could see where, on the back end of the *Witch*. The police read Asey the riot act about operating motorized vehicles when under the influence, then they dropped it. Asey's sober as a judge all day, but as soon as the sun's over the yardarm, he starts taking on the hooch," Elizabeth said frankly. "It's no wonder he was seeing ghosts! He never should have been out on the water at all that night."

Lissa's urgent question to me that first night came back starkly. "Elizabeth," I asked, "why *did* Dan take the *Sea Witch* out?"

"He got a phone call from a client. I was only

half awake, but I remember being conscious of him sitting up in bed, and hearing the rain outside, and the sound of his voice talking." Elizabeth went on methodically shelling peas. "He put down the phone, and said he had to go talk to someone right away. He was very worried; he had been for several days. I don't know why; a lawyer can't discuss a client's confidences, even with his wife."

"That's why he went out in the storm? To see a client?"

"It had to be. He wouldn't have done it for anything else. Except for family, and his family was all tucked up in bed. Dan said there was someone he had to talk to right away, that he had to take some legal action first thing in the morning and it was imperative he discuss it with this person first."

"But why the boat?"

"The client told him the road was closed. The storm had brought a tree down, and there were live electrical wires. Dan said he'd take *Sea Witch*. I tried to talk him out of it, of course. And he laughed, and kissed me, and said I was a sea captain's lady and had better get used to it. That I was to go back to sleep, and he'd be back by dawn. And so he was," Elizabeth said in a hard voice, "but not that dawn, and not the way that he'd expected. Asey Dawson is a dear soul and was Dan's good friend, but if he doesn't shut up with that business of the Watcher luring Dan to his death as a punishment for Dan's having left the sea, one of these days I'll kill him."

"It's a lie," a voice said gravely. We both jumped.

Lissa stood on the far edge of the terrace. "The Watcher doesn't kill people the way Asey says.

That's silly. The Watcher's just trying to help. But nobody pays attention."

As silently as she had appeared, she was gone again. Elizabeth looked after her and shivered. "I wish I could get her away from here. I thought it would be good for her, but it hasn't been, not since Dan died."

"You could always go back to—where was it?—Brookline?"

"Waltham. And no way. Dan and I agreed the children would grow up at Rockcove Hall, like all the other young Lancasters have before them." Elizabeth's smile flashed. "Lissa's starting to attach herself to you the way you did to me when you were small. I hoped that would happen. It's good for children to have an adult friend who's not their parent."

"Shouldn't she spend more time with kids her own age? I know this summer's going to be busy, but maybe she could phone some friends and invite them out here."

Elizabeth shook her head. "Lissa hasn't made any friends here. That's what worries—" She stopped, clapping her hand to her head. "Cindy, I'm sorry! Bill Rhodes phoned for you two hours ago, while you were in town picking up those packages! He wants you to go to the movies with him tonight. I took the liberty of accepting for you," she added dryly. "And if you're going out, we'd better eat dinner early. See if you can find Lissa, will you?" She went inside as I walked down toward the shore.

Lissa was not in sight. She's probably cut back around and gone in the house from the other side, I thought. One thing we never had to worry about was Lissa leaving the property without telling us, or falling off the rocks, or doing anything disobedient or dangerous. She was, if anything, too good. I came up from the shoreline, frowning over what Elizabeth had said about Lissa's isolation. Deborah, the golden retriever, came to meet me.

"Deborah, where's Lissa? Go find her, girl." Deborah ignored that. She was more interested in licking my hand. We came up the lawn together and, with Deborah in the lead, started to circle the mound that was the back side of the carriage house. I went around the flowering border that Deborah plowed unconcernedly through, and stopped.

The door of the carriage house was open.

Not the bolted door Elizabeth had pointed out to me. This was a low side door, so low I'd have to stoop to enter it. It was ajar, but barely. It shouldn't be open at all, was my first thought, and my second was, *Lissa*. It was like Lissa, in her silent determination, to find a child's way in and never tell anyone. Although it was Kevin who was most likely to be enthralled by the rusting old tools and things that were inside.

I had better make sure neither of them was in there now, and if either was, we'd have a serious talk about not worrying Elizabeth.

I put my hand on the door edge, and it opened easily, not creaking, as I unconsciously had expected. I bent my head and stepped over the high sill, and then my jaw dropped.

There were no rusting old tools inside, as Elizabeth had said. There was nothing but emptiness, and there was no dust. Late sunlight came faintly through a small, very dirty window on one side, but Deborah's paws, pattering over the paleness of the cement floor, left no footprints. Someone had been here.

Someone was here now, and it was not Lissa. Someone was waiting, hidden, perhaps behind that door that was a faint shape in the wood wall opposite. A sense of presence made the hairs crawl on my neck. And then fear dissolved into the ridiculous. A voice, familiar, angry, human, came behind me.

"What the devil are you doing in here?" Paul demanded.

"Looking for Lissa," I replied with dignity. "For your information, the door was open, and I got worried. If you'd use some of that energy checking up on the locks around here instead of yelling all the time or sneaking up on people—"

Paul's anger evaporated. "Sorry. So the door was open?" His eyes narrowed.

"Yes. I thought it was supposed to be locked or boarded up. Is that why you crept up on me, because you saw it open? Or does materializing without sound run in the family?"

"You didn't hear me because I have deck shoes on," Paul said absently. "Actually I was looking for you. I just brought the *Sea Witch* in. Want to come for a trial ride before I take the kids out?"

I started to say I'd love to. Then the blood rushed to my cheeks. "I can't. I'm busy."

I was going to add, Can I take a raincheck? But Paul did not give me the chance. He said curtly, "Okay, forget it," and left as abruptly as he had come.

But I couldn't forget it, though I didn't know

why the encounter stuck in my thoughts. When I came back a few days later to check on the carriage house, the little child-size door had been nailed shut.

Eight

My movie date with Bill Rhodes that Tuesday
night was strange. In a way, it was wonderful. I
felt as if I'd slipped out of the world of Rockcove
Hall and back into my life at home. Or rather, the
life I'd dreamed of having as Bill Rhodes's girlfriend.
Bill liked me. He really liked me. The electricity
we'd started that night at the prom was still there.
And yet...

After the movie we took a drive along the coast.
We were sitting in his car on the bluffs of Halibut
Point, looking out toward the winking buoys and
the sea. I stirred uneasily.

"What's wrong?" Bill asked quietly.

"I don't know." Nothing had been wrong up to
and including when he started kissing me, and I
kissed him back, and the electricity flared to life.

And then something had happened in me, something akin to what had happened before at Rockcove
Hall. Some other self took over in me, and that
self did not want Bill's arm around her, even
though Cindy Clayborne did. That self was deeply
worried. No, alarmed.

About what? The one thing I was sure of was that it had nothing whatsoever to do with Bill Rhodes.

"I'm sorry," I said lamely. I was still in his arms, but I could feel myself retreating within layer after layer of my own bone and muscle into some secret place. The way Lissa did.

"I guess I'm still thinking about everything that's been happening at Rockcove Hall. I feel like I've been caught in some kind of time warp there."

Would he laugh at that? No, he didn't. He took his arm from around me to start the engine. "Where are we going?" I asked awkwardly.

"Back to town. I want to talk to you about just that subject, and it had better be where there's plenty of lights and people—for a lot of reasons."

We went to a restaurant in one of the new motels—small, cheerful, bright lights, and plastic. "We're absolutely sure of not running into any of the locals here," Bill commented, leading the way firmly to a large secluded booth. His tone had changed so completely from out at the point that I looked at him, puzzled.

"What's this all about?"

"It's about Rockcove Hall, and the stories that are going around. I may be an outlander, but my uncle's not, and he's heard them clear down in Gloucester. I noticed how everybody clammed up when Ailsa Craig brought the subject up the night we had the cookout. Naturally that aroused my journalistic curiosity, so I did some research."

"I wish people would stop referring to gossip and then not tell me what it is," I said in exasperation.

"I'll tell you if you'll just keep your cool." Bill

glanced around to see if he could be overheard, then took out a small spiral notebook. "It seems Rockcove Hall has a ghost."

I blinked. "You sound as if you believe the stories."

"Just suspend your own disbelief until I'm finished. The first point is that the stories developed out of a grain of historic truth, the way folktales usually do. The second point is that they escalated like mad after your cousin's husband was drowned in that storm, thanks to Asey Dawson."

"I know about that," I said. "In fact, I've met him."

"I'll bet you have. But I'll bet you haven't heard his storytelling abilities in full flower. First because he apparently has to be half drunk, second because you're a member of the family and Elizabeth's friend McGovern threatened Dawson with a lawsuit if he continued telling stories. Not that that stopped him talking; it just stopped him doing it where it could get back to McGovern. He thinks Dan Lancaster was deliberately murdered. What with the police having closed the case, and Elizabeth opening Rockcove Hall as a hotel, McGovern could make a pretty good case on her behalf that Dawson was defaming her reputation, and the hall's, and destroying her ability to earn money."

"But that's crazy!" I said involuntarily. "He thinks the accident was caused by a ghost!"

"He may not be able to prove the ghost," Bill said, "but he claims he can prove it was no accident. When he's drunk enough, he starts accusing the Lancasters and the Rockport police of collusion to conceal a murder. How do you think that will go over with your paying guests?"

I gazed at him, appalled. Then I wet my lips. "What did you mean, a grain of historical truth and a ghost?"

Bill flipped notebook pages. "There really was a murder at the hall once. Or rather, a suicide someone else deliberately brought about. It was back in the early 1800s, when one of the Lancaster sea captains brought an outlander bride to Rockcove Hall."

Like Dan and Elizabeth, a voice said inside my head.

"She was very young, from Virginia somewhere." Bill was going on. "She didn't want to stay at Rockcove Hall alone. She begged her husband to let her go to sea with him, or stay with her parents in the South. But she was frail, and he was afraid the sea trip would be too hard on her. Besides, this was his first voyage as a captain, and I gather he didn't want an audience; he wanted a little woman watching for him from the widow's walk, the way Lancaster wives *always* did. Apparently pigheadedness runs in the Lancaster family."

Our eyes met involuntarily, in mutual remembrance of Paul's performance that Saturday night. "They call it strongmindedness," I murmured.

"Whatever. He sailed off, and the wife dutifully watched and waited. And apparently grew more and more delicate. She was either having second sight, or a cog slipped somewhere, depending on your point of view."

Something clogged my throat. "Go on," I said.

"Anyway, she saw something. Don't ask me what. The write-up I found in the newspaper files was just a few paragraphs, part of a column on Cape Ann tall stories. The next day she told an old servant that within the year both the husband and herself would be dead. And that very afternoon a messenger arrived with terrible news. The husband's ship had been wrecked on the reef of Norman's Woe, with all hands lost. Mrs. Lancaster didn't say a word, just went up to the widow's walk and locked the door behind her. The next morning her body was found on the rocks. She had jumped in order to join her husband in death."

I shuddered. "How awful... but it wasn't murder."

"You haven't heard the rest of the story," Bill said bluntly. "A few days later the captain himself showed up, very much alive. The story of the shipwreck had been untrue. Perhaps a deliberate lie. The townspeople tried to locate the messenger, but he was never found. The day after the captain's lady was buried in the Rockport churchyard, the captain was found dead, too, in the very same spot, with not a mark on his body to show why. And ever since then, the captain's lady is supposed to walk at the point at Rockcove Hall whenever a Lancaster's about to die."

Something was happening to me, and for no reason. My pulses pounded, and so did my heart, and my breath came erratically.

Bill didn't notice. He was turning pages in his notebook. "One of the theories about the Watcher is that she's malevolent. That she can't bear to see other happy marriages endure when hers could not, so she lures others to death by rocks or fog."

No! something in me shouted. I didn't know I'd spoken the word aloud till I saw Bill looking at me oddly.

"It's only a legend," he said gently. "But the

part about the two deaths and the inaccurate information about the shipwreck is true."

I closed my eyes. The waitress brought the coffee Bill had ordered, and he made me drink it. He was so kind, and so funny, teasing me and talking lightly about things back home, that I began coming back to normal. Or did until he leaned toward me and said very seriously, "Cindy, I want to ask you something."

I lowered my gaze, feeling fluttery, and waited. And what I heard was "Don't get angry, but I want to know. Has Elizabeth, has anybody out there said anything about seeing the Watcher at the hall the night Dan Lancaster was killed?"

I stood so swiftly, so involuntarily, that the coffee in my cup sloshed onto the table.

"I want to go home now," I said tightly.

He took me home. He didn't say anything until we reached the hall, and I said through clenched teeth, "If you ever—if you're even *thinking* about dragging all that garbage into your uncle's newspaper again, I—I think I'll kill you."

Bill was genuinely shocked. "I won't! I never intended to. I was just curious and . . . oh, let's be honest. You were scared stiff when all this started coming up that Saturday. And I'll tell you something else. Somebody else there was too. I don't know who, but I could feel the fear."

We didn't talk much more. I let him kiss me, but that's all it was, *letting*. I was like a stick of ice. And he knew it.

I let myself into the darkened house, where everyone was asleep. Or so I thought, until I reached my rooms and found Lissa and Deborah curled up together on my bed. Lissa stirred and sat up as I entered.

And something odd occurred. Something outside ourselves seemed to take over in us both. I didn't tell her she should be in bed; she didn't ask about my date. I said, totally counter to my firmest vow, "Lissa, did you see the Watcher when your father died?"

Her eyes grew enormous. She flung up an arm as if to ward off a blow and cried out, "I can't talk about her! I promised!"

In one swift movement she had slid off the bed and was out of the bedroom, through the connecting bathroom, the door to her own room slamming shut behind her.

I tried to follow, and could not. Like a sleepwalker I undressed in the dim light then crept in bed. And presently I heard the sobbing.

It was not Lissa. I do know that, because when at last I was able to free myself from the frozen stupor that imprisoned me, I went to her room, and she was sleeping soundly.

And the sobbing still went on. In the walls; above our heads.

On the bureau the glass sphere glimmered as if from its own inner light.

Nine

The next day was Wednesday, July third, the date the first paying guests would be arriving.

"What a lucky break, having the Fourth of July on a Thursday," Elizabeth kept saying. Most workplaces would stay closed on Friday, too, giving people a long holiday weekend. We already had five rooms rented, and by early afternoon the chamber of commerce had referred reservations for the remaining five. Seven couples, three of them with children that would occupy two-room suites like mine; two men, each traveling alone; one woman. Some would get here in time for Wednesday dinner, the others were expected later in the evening or on the Fourth.

"You *must* be here on call all day, and presentable!" Elizabeth told Paul more than once, and he kept retorting, "*I know!*" with increasing irritation. The Rockport taxi, to put it charitably, was undependable.

There was no tranquility at Rockcove Hall that day. Martha and Ella were preparing food for dinner and getting in the carpenters' way. Asey

Dawson was underfoot, seeming to do little but accomplishing a great deal. He was cold sober, and all he talked about was the upcoming Fourth of July parade and the madhouse that would result from all the dangfool day trippers dumping themselves on Bearskin Neck and the adjacent beaches.

There was so much I had to think about, and my mind did so while my feet ran errands, and my hands made beds and put lavender-scented soap and nosegays of flowers in the guest rooms. My voice told Elizabeth to calm down, everything was fine, but my mind had no such certainty.

To be honest, I wasn't thinking straight. My mine was like a television set, running and rerunning pictorial images of all Bill had told me last night about the hall, of all the things that had happened since my arrival that I didn't understand.

Bill. I owed him an apology for the way I'd acted, but I didn't have time to call him. I didn't know what to say. I didn't know how to explain my actions, my responses, even to myself.

At last it was four-thirty, and the carpenters departed. Ella set tables on the dining porch. Elizabeth and I and the children hurried upstairs to shower and dress while Paul, glowering but immaculate, paced back and forth by the phone. We were going to eat in the gray-and-white dining room before any of the guests arrived.

I was just stepping out of the shower when the phone rang. A minute later Paul screeched out of the driveway in Elizabeth's car, headed for town to pick someone up. The phone rang again. I picked it up and found Elizabeth had already answered in her bedroom and was giving some man detailed directions on how to drive here from Gloucester without encountering a traffic jam. Then a car pulled into the parking lot beneath my window.

Elizabeth wasn't downstairs. *I* wasn't downstairs. I wasn't even dressed, but I dove into my copper-colored cotton dress quickly, ran a hasty brush over my hair, and hurried down.

A middle-aged man was standing in the sitting room, his back to me as he looked at some brochures spread on the center table. He straightened as he heard my footsteps.

"Good evening. My name's Martin; I have a reservation." He broke off, looking at me intently. Then he smiled, an infectious smile that made him look like a Buddha or a cherub. "And you, my dear young lady, must be a Lancaster."

I smiled back involuntarily. "Sorry, I'm from *Mrs.* Lancaster's side of the family. If you'll sign the register, please." He did so in minuscule calligraphy, squinting at it through thick rimless glasses. Albert Henry Martin. The old-fashioned name went with the rest of him. He must be a painter, for he carried an easel and paint box along with his battered leather satchel.

Before I could ask him, two more cars pulled in. Mr. and Mrs. J. Wallace, and Mr. and Mrs. T. Curtis. Young couples, apparently friends, with three preschoolers between them. They got the two suites in the center block of the second floor. Mr. Martin was supposed to have the double room between them. I wondered how he was going to like being so near young children. I offered him a third-floor room instead, and he leaped at it.

By then Elizabeth had come down, and the children. The four-year-old Wallace boy stared at Kevin with fascination. Lissa took one look at the

Curtis baby and his toddler sister, and for the first time that summer looked totally happy. Her offer to sit with the children while their parents had dinner was immediately accepted.

I showed everybody to their rooms. Elizabeth manned the front desk. Paul returned, bringing an aristocratic-looking white-haired widow. The phone rang, and he left for town again. Mr. Wallace and Mr. Curtis asked about fishing charters. The chamber of commerce called to see if we had any vacancies for Thursday night. I was still saying no when Mr. Martin started asking all sorts of questions about painting sites. I referred him to Elizabeth. An overdressed middle-aged couple named Gass walked in, demanding help with their luggage.

"I'm sorry, it will be a few minutes. Our porter's picking up someone at the station—" The phone shrilled again and I scooped it up with an abrupt "Yes?"

"Is this a bad time to call?" It was Bill.

I turned away from the guests, my face scarlet. "I'm sorry. I was going to call you to apologize."

"No need. I can hear you're busy. Any chance you can go to the parade with me tomorrow?"

"I don't know. Meet you if I can. Come swim in the afternoon if you want, and stay for supper." I put the phone down and concentrated on being gracious to the annoyed Gasses, but it was an effort.

Being innkeepers was going to be every bit as stressful as Ailsa Craig had predicted.

Somehow, the early evening passed with relative smoothness, due mainly to Martha Gibbs's cooking. Her creamy fish chowder was a dream, and her lobsters (special order, extra charge) were in demand. Elizabeth and I never did sit down in the dining room; we grabbed food in passing in the kitchen. And the twilight view across the cove, with lights coming on slowly on Bearskin Neck and the green light flashing over on Straitsmouth Island, was all the guests could desire.

Afterward some of the guests drove into town; others strolled on the lawns or watched TV. Mr. Gass wanted to be taken out for a harbor cruise. "You advertised free boat rides," he said aggressively.

"Not after dark. On clear mornings only, and not on weekends," Paul said shortly. Mr. Gass wasn't pleased.

Eventually Elizabeth was able to get most of the visitors downstairs to the lounge to watch TV. The Gasses had complaints about that too. "No cable? You mean we won't get to see any of the movie channels?"

"We're planning to rent a VCR and show movies Saturday night," answered Elizabeth, who had planned no such thing. She looked at me over Mrs. Gass's lacquered hairdo and rolled her eyes.

"The regular network shows are just fine for me," Mrs. Wilson, the elderly widow, said comfortably. "How about you, Mr. Martin?"

"Eh? Oh, of course. Of course. Only watch when I'm on vacations, you know. Reading's more my line." He had his finger in a fat book of Massachusetts lore. "Is it true some of the Salem witches lived in Rockport?"

"The tourist brochure says that, but I've never run across any evidence," Elizabeth said, smiling. "You'll have to go over to Salem for that. It isn't far."

Mr. Martin looked as if he were going to say something more, but he didn't.

So we watched TV, all of us except Paul, who went to check on Lissa and Kevin. Steve McGovern telephoned, and Ailsa, too, to ask Elizabeth how things were going. They would both be over tomorrow night for dinner. I could hear these conversations going on, softly, in the closet Elizabeth had converted to a telephone booth—it had a pay phone for the guests and a house extension that took incoming calls only.

Elizabeth was still on the phone with Ailsa when the electricity began to flicker.

It was the same thing that had happened on my first night, only it was not as noticeable at the start because everyone was looking at the television program. I may have been the only one who saw the room's two lamps dim, and realized that it was one of those brownouts causing the snow on the TV screen. Then, just as Elizabeth emerged from her talk with Ailsa, all the lights went out.

Mrs. Gass, predictably, screamed. "*Mom!* Lissa shouted from upstairs. I heard Paul's footsteps pounding down. "It's just a momentary power shutdown from overload." Elizabeth was already lighting the room's two oil lamps. Sure enough, the lights came on again dimly. The TV screen lit up. Then the lights lowered again as a sound like a gunshot and a burst of sparks exploded on the terrace.

"Somebody's setting fireworks!" Paul dove for the door. "*Asey?* What the devil do you think you're doing? I don't care what you promised Kevin, put those things away and get in here!"

The lights and the TV came on full power again.

Then, though the TV picture remained clear, the lamps dimmed. Mrs. Wilson looked at Mr. Martin slyly. "Perhaps your Salem witches are playing games with us."

Mrs. Gass yelped, Mr. Martin remarked portentously that stranger things had happened, and Mr. Gass told him crossly not to joke about things like that.

"What makes you think I'm joking?" Mr. Martin retorted, deliberately baiting him.

"Rockcove Hall don't have no Salem ghosts." Asey had arrived in time to overhear, and his implication, to my ears at least, was all too unmistakable. With one mind Elizabeth, Paul, and I mobilized.

"Asey, come upstairs. I want to ask you something about the *Sea Witch* engine." Paul steered him toward the stairs.

"Elizabeth can't we—" I asked.

Elizabeth, completing my thought, said loudly, "Wouldn't everyone like some coffee? Or some iced tea?"

"That sounds like a great idea. Can we help? And can my husband take one of those lamps upstairs to check the children?" Mrs. Curtis stood up, smiling and blessedly calm.

At that moment the lights came on again. The TV blared. And although Asey had shut and locked the door behind him, I felt a sudden cold current of air against my neck.

I swung my head around sharply toward the door. It was ajar.

No one else noticed. I could scarcely be sure of what I'd seen myself, because almost immediately there was another of those firecracker blasts outside, and an echoing thunder from the sky, and the electric lights blacked out. Elizabeth groaned.

"That does it! I'm sorry, but a power line must have come down somewhere. Why don't we all go up to the Walnut Room, and—"

She was interrupted by Mrs. Gass's scream.

"The lines aren't down! Look!" Mrs. Gass's shaking finger pointed at the television screen. The picture and sound had vanished, but the tube was lighted, though it showed only wavy lines.

"There's your witch!" Mr. Martin said with relish, peering at a darkening shape that was forming in the center of the screen. The picture focused, clarified.

Elizabeth strode over and snapped the set off. "I *am* sorry," she said in a perfectly normal voice. "We obviously have a crossed line somewhere. Something must have happened to the set when the electricians were working here last week." She led the way to the stairs and the others followed, talking cheerfully.

I couldn't move. I stood rooted to the spot, staring at the blank gray screen, while my heart and pulses pounded and dizziness assailed me. For in that split-second I had seen, and recognized, what everyone else could not.

It had not been just some "shape" on the screen, or a double image from some other program. It had not been Mr. Martin's wished-for Salem witch. The figure that had looked back at me, looked at *me*, had been the young woman in the white nightgown with burnished hair who had gazed at me so sadly out of my bedroom mirror.

Ten

My rooms, when I finally reached them, were a haven. I locked the doors, feeling foolish. Surely a ghost—if there *was* any ghost—would not be put off by a bolted door! But I slept easier all the same.

I awoke while it was still dark to the sound of voices in the corridor outside. Had guests (I could guess which) come prowling? I unbolted the door, opened it a crack, and found the voices belonged to Paul and Kevin.

"What are you—"

"Shh, don't wake Lissa," Paul whispered hastily. It was the first time he'd spoken to me voluntarily since I'd turned down his invitation for the boat ride.

Kevin didn't know that. He said blithely in what he thought was a whisper, "Cindy, c'mon! Paul's going to take the *Sea Witch* out!"

"Won't Lissa be disappointed?"

Paul frowned a warning to me, but when he spoke, it was to Kevin. "Cindy's probably not interested in sailing at this hour." That's what he said; what he meant was that I wouldn't be interested in going out for a sail with him.

"Oh, yes, I am," I said promptly. I had reasons of my own for wanting to explore the *Sea Witch*.

"Then get dressed fast and meet us on the dock," Paul ordered.

If that's the mood he's in, I thought, it isn't going to be a great sail. I dove into a T-shirt, jeans, and sneakers and hurried downstairs, avoiding a creaking stair tread.

The *Sea Witch* rolled quietly at her mooring pole a few yards from shore, and Paul was waiting with a dinghy. "I don't want to risk waking the tourists with an engine," he said sardonically.

"Why do you hate the idea of paying guests so much?" I asked as he cast off and began to row.

"Because Rockcove Hall's been a family home for two hundred years. In *my* family. I'm sorry, I know it's Elizabeth's now." The dawn freshness and the water's spell seemed to be softening his mood. "But I don't like having it ruined by strangers tramping around asking stupid questions. What do you bet that Martin creep tries to con Elizabeth out of some of the antiques?"

"They're not ruining it. They're making it possible for you all to stay there. Or would you rather see the hall sold for real estate development the way Ailsa Craig keeps recommending?" I asked pointedly.

I had him there. "We wouldn't be in this mess," Paul said, reddening, "if—" He shot a glance at Kevin, who was all ears. "Ahoy, mate! Prepare to make fast and board!"

We bumped against the *Sea Witch*. Kevin passed a coil of rope to Paul, who secured the dinghy to the mooring pole, swung himself up onto the *Sea Witch*, and turned to help us up the ladder. Kevin scrambled up like a monkey, and I followed.

Paul—or had it been Dan?—must have started teaching Kevin seamanship early. The two of them had the cruiser's sails up in short order, Paul cast off, and soon we were moving out of the cove in a fresh breeze.

"It's a shame for Lissa to miss this," I exclaimed, gazing across the spangled waters at the Bearskin Neck buildings glowing in the dawn.

"Lissa would have a spaz attack." Kevin gave me a funny look. "Don't you know that?"

"Mate! Go below and forage for some breakfast," Paul ordered. When the boy had vanished, he looked at me. "Kevin's right. You're Miss Sensitivity, according to Elizabeth. How come you haven't picked up that Lissa has a phobia about the *Sea Witch*? She won't look at it and she won't come near it. She can't stand hearing it or her father talked about, and she's furious with her mother and me because Elizabeth let me repair the boat. Not that Elizabeth could have stopped me. Dan left me the *Sea Witch*."

"How come you're furious at Elizabeth and me?" I countered.

"I'm not furious at you." Paul glanced at me, then away. "You did a good job last night. You kept your head. I thought for a while we were going to have a real mess on our hands."

"What do *you* think caused that—that business?"

"Brownout, wires down, and crossed channels. Didn't you hear?" Paul's voice had an edge to it. "Or do you prefer the ghost theory?"

We both stopped talking as Kevin's head popped

up from the galley. He tossed us each an apple and flourished a bag of doughnuts. Paul had been well prepared. He was so different where the children were concerned, I thought.

While Kevin hung over the stern, tossing doughnut crumbs to the wheeling gulls, I went to stand by Paul. "What did you start to say, you Lancasters wouldn't be in a money mess *if*. If what?"

"If Dan had been here at the hall, managing his own money instead of being all wrapped up in becoming a rich city lawyer somewhere else. Oh, sure, he may have made more there," Paul anticipated my thought, "but he wouldn't have needed much here. He owned the hall. There was my grandfather's boating business. Dan knew I wanted that, but oh, no, he had to go and sell it. *I* had to go to Harvard, not be a boat bum. He never asked me what I wanted. He was too busy listening to Elizabeth." Paul took a deep breath.

I was speechless at first from the force of his words. Why was he so defensive? "I asked you before," I said after a moment. "But you didn't answer. Why do you hate Elizabeth?"

Paul rubbed spray off his face with his sleeve. "I don't hate her. I hate what her being an outlander did to us. To Dan. Dan would have been satisfied to stay here if it hadn't been for her."

"You can't know that. And he did come back."

"Sure. After our grandfather died here alone. After all the natives thought we'd deserted the hall for good, and Dan had let the money he'd been piling up get lost in crazy investment schemes."

"So maybe he wasn't as smart at investing as he was at earning," I said bluntly. "That's not his wife's fault. And he certainly must have expected to live for years. Or are you trying to blame his accident on Elizabeth too?"

"All I'm saying," Paul said deliberately, turning the *Sea Witch* back toward the cove, "is that the Dan I grew up with would never have had an accident with a cruiser this size on rocks he knew like his own hand, in the middle of the night."

"There was a storm! He went out because a client needed him—that is what lawyers are supposed to do, you know!" All at once we were in the middle of a cut-down session again. "It was an accident!"

Paul looked straight at me. "*Was* it?"

I caught my breath. "The next thing, you'll be saying it was a ghost, like Asey Dawson does."

He didn't ask how I'd found that out. He didn't defend Asey, who I knew by now was like an old uncle to him. He gave me another of those level looks and asked in a dead-serious voice, "What do you think? Really?"

I was saved from answering by a small speed-boat filled with tourists that cut across our prow. Paul swore and jerked the *Sea Witch* aside sharply as the tourists shook their fists at us and shouted.

"Might as well start the engine," Paul muttered when they were gone. "The harbor's getting crowded. I want to get home before there's any more craziness." He and Kevin furled the sails and we made for the hall rapidly, cutting around the pleasure craft that were beginning to dot the waters.

We were well into daylight now. I realized guiltily that Elizabeth had been expecting me to help with breakfast, but when I hurried to the kitchen, she just glanced at me briefly, then went on piling blueberry muffins in a basket.

Martha rolled her eyes at me when Elizabeth had left. "Don't worry. Mrs. Lancaster's working up a fret for nothing. Didn't sleep much, did she?" I looked at her, startled, wondering if she'd already heard about last night's excitement, but her face was blank. "You run upstairs and clean up. Ella will help wait tables. Everything's fine."

I could, I discovered, use a good bit of cleaning up. I took a fast shower and ran a comb through my hair after first rubbing the steam off the bathroom mirror. It made me think uncomfortably of that—that doppelganger in my bedroom mirror.

I had met that word, *doppelganger,* meaning "other walker" or shadow self, in an English lit story last year. At that time the idea had seemed deliciously scary, though farfetched. I had never expected—I brought myself up short. What was happening to my mind, anyway?

A second image did appear in my mirror while I stood there, but it wasn't mine. It was Lissa's, with that deliberating, unchildlike look in her eyes.

"You were out in the *Sea Witch,* weren't you?"

"Yes, I was," I said matter-of-factly. "Does that bother you?"

Lissa just looked at me, as if I'd slipped a notch in her estimation. "Something happened downstairs last night, didn't it? Paul wouldn't tell me."

"What makes you think anything happened?"

She gave me another of those pitying glances, and vanished as silently as she had come.

Fortunately none of the guests on the dining porch was thinking about last night. Everyone was chatting excitedly about the Independence Day celebrations. Rockport put on an old-fashioned

Fourth complete with a parade of bands and floats, various afternoon activities for the whole family, and a concert. It would all wind up with a giant bonfire and fireworks. Somehow, Elizabeth had succeeded in convincing all the guests that lunch in town would be more fun than at the hall, so we would have one less meal to prepare and serve. A traditional clambake and lobster feast was to be our dinner menu.

"I'll stay here to receive today's arrivals. You take the children to the parade," Elizabeth told me. "No, really. I'd rather be here in peace and quiet and steal a swim."

"Is Paul going?"

Elizabeth laughed. "He wouldn't be caught dead in Bearskin Neck or Dock Square with all those tourists!" In the sunshine, in her crisp pale blue linen dress, she was her old serene self.

So I took Kevin and Lissa into town—on bicycles, to avoid a parking situation—and we saw Bill Rhodes there. If he was disconcerted that I had two chaperons, he didn't show it. He treated us all to hot dogs and fried clams for lunch, followed by double milk shakes, a dreadful-sounding but yummy combination. We bought balloons. We bought ice cream sandwiches. We watched the parade and got sunburned and laughed a lot. But Bill and I didn't speak about Rockcove Hall or the Watcher.

Bill had his car with him, and we loaded our bicycles into the hatchback for a crowded, fun ride back to Rockcove Hall. Preparations for the clambake were under way, with Paul and Asey presiding over the fire pit. Bill took one look at Paul's expression and sensibly did not offer to help. Instead, he and Lissa put themselves in charge of keeping the guest children, including an obnoxious eight-year-old boy who'd arrived in our absence, out of harm's way.

It wasn't that easy keeping Albert Henry Martin in line. He inserted himself into everything, succeeded in burning himself with the hot stones and steam (Mr. Gass advised him to sue), and proceeded to become very chummy with old Asey.

Ailsa, arriving with blueberry cobbler as a dessert contribution, took a look and raised her eyebrows. "If you're going to let that old coot inflict himself on the paying guests, you're asking for problems."

"Asey's my local color," Elizabeth said calmly. "He's cold sober; I've already checked. Anyway, Mr. Martin's an artist who's interested in local history. He'd probably like a half-crocked Asey even better."

"That's not *Albert Henry* Martin?" Ailsa groaned. "I thought there was something familiar about that plaid rump facing me."

My ears perked up. "You know him?"

"More than I want to and less than he would like. He's an amateur dabbler who thinks he's a professional because he occasionally sells a pretty picture for less than the cost of his art supplies," Ailsa answered bluntly. "He turns up at showings and professional association meetings around New York. He's either eccentric or cracked, depending on your charity. I hope he isn't staying here long."

"Two weeks."

"Tell Elizabeth not to expect to see much of me for the next fourteen days."

Mr. Martin knew who Ailsa was all right, and

the minute he spotted her, he zeroed in. That at least got him away from Asey and the fire pit.

We ate on the lower lawn, near the sea-washed rocks, as dusk was falling. It was magical. I gazed around me at the assembled guests, and for a moment I saw myself and the others as through the lens of a camera, or through a painter's eye. Elizabeth at a round table with Steve McGovern on one side of her and Mrs. Wilson on the other. Mr. Ikawa, our Japanese tourist, snapping pictures while Mr. Martin gave advice. The other guests scattered around at the various tables, the children now subdued from all the day's excitement.

Except for our clothes, we could have been celebrating a New England Fourth in any year since 1776. The sights and tastes were the same, the scents and sound. As darkness deepened, fireworks spangled the sky from across the cove.

I became aware of a tension in the air, and it had nothing whatever to do with the Watcher. I gradually realized that it was because Bill was on one side of me and Paul was on the other. And that I was not the only one of us who felt it. Paul's voice grew louder and more commanding. Bill bent his head to me and began talking about experiences we'd shared back home, about the newspaper—things Paul had no part in. At one point I felt a pull from another direction and looked over, startled. Lissa was regarding me with grave, measuring eyes.

"Walk me to my car," Bill said when it was time for him to go. I stood leaning against the Honda and he stood before me, his hands resting on the car roof, shielding me apart from the others. "I don't want to spoil today, but I have to say this. I

need to talk to you. Soon. About what I asked you
the other night that scared you so much."

"Bill, I—"

All at once I felt cold. A shudder shook me.
Bill's arms pulled me tight, and then he kissed
me. "Don't think about it now," he said huskily
when he lifted his head at last. "Go to sleep, and
try not to be so frightened. Whatever's going on
here, you're not alone in it, I promise."

He kissed me again and got into his car. I
walked slowly to the hall door, feeling dazed.

I almost screamed as a dark form emerged from
the shrubbery.

"It's me," Paul said swiftly. "What were you and
Rhodes talking about? Was he trying to pump you
about Rockcove Hall?"

I *was* frightened, as Bill had said. But as I
looked into Paul's angry eyes, a kind of automatic
pilot took over in me.

"What makes you think the Lancaster family
ghost is the only thing that would make Bill want
to talk to me?" I asked deliberately.

Paul stared at me, breathing hard, then turned
on his heel and plunged down toward the shore.

I groped for the door handle and went inside.
And a presence was there waiting for me. I felt it
with every nerve ending in my body, but I was not
afraid. Whatever, whoever this *energy* in Rockcove
Hall belonged to, it was there particularly for me,
and I knew it meant me the opposite of harm.

Eleven

At breakfast Friday morning the Gasses were demanding their anticipated cruise around the harbor. "Don't give me that line about how you won't take the boat out on weekends. You took it out yesterday. Thought you were pretty smart, sneaking out, didn't you?" Mr. Gass thrust his face at Paul belligerently. "Well, we saw you from our windows when you came back. That brochure we were sent promised boat rides, and if you think you can take the hotel staff out and not the customers, you can think again. What do you call that thing, the *Sea Witch*? We're entitled to a ride in it, and we're going to get it."

"No, you won't." The words were so sudden, and so unexpected coming from Lissa, that I was not the only one who jumped. I caught at her arm, but she paid no attention. "The *Sea Witch* is my father's boat, and you don't belong on it!"

"Is that so? Well, your old man doesn't seem to be in evidence, and we're paying plenty." Mr. Gass turned on Elizabeth. "If you want to keep your customers, you'd better keep your children in line. And you'd better provide what you advertise, or I'm reporting you to the Better Business Bureau."

A muscle twitched in Elizabeth's temple, but her voice was level. "We'll all go. We should be able to circle the harbor before the crowds go out. Paul, prep the outboard." Her eyes flicked around the room. "Anyone else who would like to come, please be down at the dock in twenty minutes in rubber-soled shoes. This will be the only boat ride all weekend. Kevin, Lissa, if you're finished eating, go put on your sneakers."

"*No.*" Lissa's eyes filled with panic.

"I said all of us," Elizabeth repeated inexorably. I understood what she was doing. Lissa had to deal with the *Sea Witch* and Dan's death once and for all, just as Elizabeth had. Postponing that reality only made it harder. But I ached for Lissa all the same.

So I rode out to the gently rolling *Sea Witch* again, this time in a power boat with my arms around a rigid Lissa. Paul had to make three trips to transport everyone who wanted to go. Elizabeth was right about that too; better to satisfy the Gasses and have the equally dreadful eight-year-old Mike Riley get a boat ride now with several adults along than have them pestering us—or, worse, prowling around the *Sea Witch*—all weekend.

The trip was not as bad as it might have been. Mr. Martin sat in the stern and sketched, and Mike Riley, after inspecting the cruiser top to bottom, hung over the artist's shoulder but was not rebuffed. Mrs. Wilson sat with Elizabeth and Lissa and kept them engaged in cheerful conversation. Lissa seemed to relax a little once we were under way. Mr. Ikawa and two other men took pictures. I circulated, playing the role of hostess. Elizabeth had had the foresight to bring a basket of Martha's Danish pastries, and thermoses of orange juice and coffee.

Mike Riley, tiring of Mr. Martin, threw crumbs and then torn-up bits of paper napkin to the gulls. "You can't do that," Lissa said coldly. "That's littering."

"I can too if I want to!" He danced in front of her, waving a napkin tauntingly beneath her nose. She grabbed it.

"No, you can't! Not from my father's boat!"

"Yeah? Your father's not here! He got drownded because he couldn't sail this tub right—"

I tried to pull Lissa away, but I couldn't. She was on him like a cat, screaming and flailing, forcing him against the rail. He fought back, screaming too. It all happened so fast. One moment they were struggling, the next Mike was falling over into the water. Paul, holding the wheel he dared not leave, shouted for Elizabeth, and she was over the side in one swift dive while Mrs. Wilson and I swept up Lissa.

Elizabeth had Mike by the chin, though he was fighting her. She pulled him with her toward the *Sea Witch*. Paul had cut the motor and was keeping the boat steady. Somebody found blankets in the main cabin. Somebody helped Mr. Riley haul his son up from Elizabeth's arms. Somebody else helped Elizabeth up the ladder. Somebody wrapped the two of them in blankets. I was totally involved with Lissa, who was practically catatonic.

Mr. Martin hovered helplessly. "I'm so sorry. I told the boy the story because I thought he'd find it interesting. I never thought—"

"You didn't think, period," Paul said roughly. "Now, sit down, everybody, and stay put! I want to get back to shore fast!"

He gunned the motor. Above us the sky was turning an ominous gray.

By the time we reached the mooring pole, rain was already starting to fall. Paul took Elizabeth and the Rileys into land first, and for once the Gasses had no complaint. They and Mr. Martin huddled under the awning, looking subdued.

The first thing Elizabeth did when she reached the hall, probably even before taking off her wet clothes, was phone Steve and ask about insurance coverage. The second was to apologize to the Rileys, who for a change considered their precious boy was in the wrong. I found this out afterward from Kevin. At the time I was preoccupied with Lissa, who moved like an automaton and would not talk, not even to me, not even when we were cozily ensconced in my rooms with Deborah licking Lissa comfortingly and a fire lit to ward off the clammy chill.

"I don't blame you a bit," I said at last. "But Lissa, what you did was *wrong*. You know it. And it's wrong to—to try to make Rockcove Hall and the *Sea Witch* into a memorial to your dad. He's gone, and that's terrible for you, but life goes on. Your father would want it to. Lissa, do you understand what I'm saying?"

Lissa gave me one of those unfathomable looks. "*You* don't understand. They'll have to pay for this." And that was the last thing she would say.

Lunch was uncomfortable despite Mrs. Wilson's efforts to induce a pleasant atmosphere. We had to set up the buffet inside, for rain flooded the terrace. By midafternoon the rain was coming down so hard that no one wanted to venture out, and people were getting bored. Mike recovered enough to make a nuisance of himself, which at least had the advantage of driving Mr. Martin to his room. The others read, or watched TV, or played cards, and the Gasses complained.

Steve arrived in a slicker and was closeted first with the Rileys, then with Elizabeth. "They're not going to sue," Martha said comfortably. "You can stop worrying."

I looked up from the vegetables I was peeling. "How do you know?"

She snorted. "One thing, Mr. McGovern can talk anybody into or out of anything. Second thing, I was walking past the sitting room, where he was talking to the Rileys, and I heard. Too bad that brat didn't drown, or some other people I could mention, 'stead of a decent man like Dan Lancaster."

She jerked her head toward the kitchen door. Mrs. Gass stood there, her face indignant. "Is there something I can do for you?" I asked, controlling myself.

"You can get that leak over my bed fixed right away, that's what!"

I followed her upstairs with a sinking heart.

The Gasses had what had been Dan and Elizabeth's master bedroom, in a lovely suite with windows toward the sea. Pale blue satin swagged the lace-hung windows and draped the bed. Water was seeping in down the satin-striped wallpaper, why, I didn't know, for the room was not on the top floor. I interrupted Steve and Elizabeth and reported the leak, and Elizabeth sighed. "I'd better call

Asey and hope he's sober. He's the only one who
might be available today."

"You'd better come down and act as social hostess too. The natives are getting restless, especially
Mrs. G."

Asey came, and was at least sober enough to
find the leak and stop it. Elizabeth persuaded the
Gasses to come down to the Walnut Room and
have tea before the fire. That was a good idea, for
by now everyone was restless. No one but I, I
think, could tell the strain Elizabeth was under.
Presiding behind a silver teapot and offering little
cakes originally meant for dinner, Elizabeth worked
her particular magic. Presently the room began to
relax. There was the clink of china, and the sound
of laughter. Elizabeth had even been able to get
Lissa to come down.

"*Here* you all are! Charming, charming!" Mr.
Martin bustled in, carrying a wrapped object over
which he hovered. "Oh, yes, thank you, dear lady.
Three lumps, please." He propped the object against
the bookshelves and loitered, elaborately casual.

Mrs. Wilson gave me a mischievous look. "You've
been painting, haven't you, Mr. Martin? Do let us
see."

"Oh, no, no . . . well, if you insist." He unveiled
the wet canvas proudly.

There was a silence. Ailsa had been right, his
painting was not very professional. But that wasn't
all.

"My goodness, Mr. Martin," Mrs. Wilson said
lightly, "you've been riding your other hobby horse,
haven't you? That is supposed to be a spirit of
some kind, isn't it?"

Mr. Martin beamed. "Not just a spirit. The

captain's lady. Rockcove Hall's own private and particular ghost." He tittered. "Maybe this is the lady who was playing lights out with us last night. I wouldn't know; I haven't seen her in her spirit form. Some of those present may have a closer acquaintance with her."

He looked straight at me with an indescribable expression, and tittered again.

"There's no such thing as ghosts!" Mike Riley jeered. "Everybody knows that!"

"Speak for yourself, young man." Mr. Martin was unruffled. "I've just been having a most interesting conversation with a genuine native, lineage goes back clear to the Salem witch trials." He transferred his attention to Elizabeth. "What's his name? Dawkins? Dawson? He tells me the night your husband was killed there was a genuine supernatural manifestation—"

I knew I wasn't the only one who felt the current run through the room. Mr. Riley laughed. "Mike's right. There aren't any real ghosts. But it's a riot what some people believe. Did you hear the one about—" He was off on a ribald story. At least it turned the subject off Dan's death and the captain's lady. But I had seen the expressions on certain faces—Elizabeth's, Lissa's, Paul's, Steve's. Who else had seen them? I wondered.

The electricity began its familiar trick of browning out. "The captain's lady!" Mrs. Gass said theatrically, and laughed.

I took hold of Lissa's hand and gripped it warningly. She kept silent. Mrs. Wilson cleared her throat. "Perhaps we should be thinking up some appropriately antique activities for this evening. If this storm keeps up, no one will want to go out, but the electricity probably *will*, which means no TV." She eyed Mr. Martin sternly. "And no telling ghost stories. They're fascinating, but too stimulating for the children."

"I was thinking perhaps a nineteenth-century dinner party," Elizabeth said calmly. "We have kerosene lamps and candles if the lines go down. We have trunks of period clothing in the attic if you'd enjoy dressing up. After dinner there could be round games, or music if anyone plays piano."

There was a chorus of appreciation and some volunteers. "I'll unlock the attic. Give me half an hour to locate things for you, and then come up."

When we reached the third-floor hall thirty minutes later, we found a row of oil lamps lit and waiting. "One for each family, and carried by adults only," Elizabeth instructed. "I'd prefer the children not go up at all." Steve McGovern organized a game of hide-and-seek for them, confined to the public rooms. The rest of us climbed the steep stairs.

The attic was a magical place, straight out of old stories or fairy tales. The main beams were tree trunks still wearing their bark. Several chests and boxes had been dragged to the middle of the floor, and the guests fell upon them rapturously. I could hear two of the women exclaiming over the quality of the old lace.

I stood still, momentarily dazed. No wonder, I thought, considering everything that had gone on that day. I'd better find something I could wear, then try to steal a nap.

My feet moved me toward a far corner. A small trunk sat there, surrounded by old books. I meant to say "Elizabeth, can I look here?" but I didn't. I just put my hand out and tried the lock, and the trunk opened. I turned back layers of dark garments as if something was guiding me, moving my hands down to a dress of soft coppery silk, and I pulled it out.

Like a sleepwalker I folded it carefully, shut the lid, and went back to my cousin, saying faintly, "Is it all right if I wear this?"

"Yes, if you want to," Elizabeth answered absently. She was helping the men try on Victorian frock coats.

I went down to my own rooms, but not to nap. I stripped off my slacks and T-shirt, and let the silk dress slip down over my bare body. It fit as though made for me. I gazed in the mirror and was seeing that other self—myself but older. I was I, Cindy Clayborne, and I was a captain's lady, young and in love.

Perhaps I should have jerked the dress off right then and run. I did not. Could not.

What I did was sit down in the rocker by the small fire, and brush my hair, and let my mind float free. And where it went, what it saw, I could not later say. But there was a deep serenity in me as I went downstairs.

It had become dinnertime. No one had called me. As I descended the main staircase, Ella rang the gong. Candles burned in the Walnut Room and in the gray-and-white family dining room, where the table had been extended to its fullest length and covered with old lace. We were all to dine together.

The electricity was still functioning, but dimly. The others were gathering, admiring each other's clothes. Elizabeth was regal in blue-gray taffeta with hoops. Even the children were all there, dressed in their best. . . . Elizabeth had not wanted Lissa upstairs baby-sitting in case the electricity went off completely, no doubt.

The doorbell rang, and I went to it. Bill stood there, dripping rain. "Hope my blue suit and some shirt ruffles will do for a costume. I didn't have time enough to dig up anything. You look terrific."

I blinked. "What are you doing here?"

Bill looked at me in astonishment. "I got a message at the paper that somebody'd phoned inviting me to Rockcove Hall for a whaling-days dinner. It was you, wasn't it?"

I shook my head. "I wanted to, but I never had a chance to ask Elizabeth's permission. Too much has been going on. She must have invited you herself, to surprise me."

Bill gave me a thoughtful look. "I'm glad to be here anyway. We have to have a serious talk. Tonight, if possible. I need to know what you're not telling me."

The gong rang again. Bill tucked my arm through his, and with the others we moved to the dining room. Elizabeth went to one end of the table; Paul started toward the other. Bill held a chair for me at one side, and I began to sit, then halted. Paul had reached the host chair, to find Steve there first.

For a minute their eyes locked. Then Steve, with a smile at Elizabeth, pulled the chair out and sat down. Paul stared at him. Then, his face a thundercloud, he sat down by Lissa. Lissa was not sitting; she stood at her place, gazing straight at Steve.

On Lissa's other side Ailsa stood motionless.

Why, she's in love with McGovern—the thought struck me suddenly, though I had no overt proof.

I looked away quickly, and felt Mr. Martin's eyes practically boring into me. When mine met them, he swept me a little bow and smirked.

Ella served the first course, a mixture of native berries in stemmed glass dishes.

As she served the soup, the lights went out. Mike Riley guffawed. "So we dine by candlelight. How delightful," Mrs. Wilson said placidly.

One of the candle flames flickered and went out. Mrs. Gass gave a muted shriek.

"Nothing to worry about," her husband said heartily. "That draft from the porch window did it."

But there are no windows open, my mind said silently.

Elizabeth spoke. "Lissa, check the windows, will you please? One may be open a crack."

Lissa obeyed silently. A moment later another candle went out as if snuffed.

That was one thing I noticed, and remembered. The flame did not blow sideways, although there was indeed a draft coming from behind me. It just—went out. And then the other candles in the room went out also, one after another.

Just before the last flame died, Mike Riley's chair lurched away from the table toward the far wall, throwing him to the floor as a large silver pitcher on the sideboard sailed through the air.

Steve McGovern was on his feet, running around the table to Elizabeth. He swept her into his arms just as the room went black.

Twelve

There was a cold draft. There were the sounds of stumbling and shuffling. There was screaming. The silver pitcher crashed against the wall and fell to the floor. I heard the crash and the metallic ring. I could not see it. The room was as black as night.

"Stay put!" Bill said into my ear. I heard his chair sliding back, heard his footsteps cross the floor. Sideboard drawers opened and closed as someone searched for matches.

Mr. Curtis produced a lighter. By the dim glow I saw faces: Mrs. Gass, still screaming as her husband tried to quiet her. Elizabeth and Steve, locked in each other's arms, with Kevin pressed silently against them. Ailsa, the skeptic, looking as though she'd had a glimpse of hell and had seen the ghost of Rockcove Hall.

The candles refused to light.

The iron plant stand in the bow window suddenly tipped crazily, spilling its pot of geraniums to the ground. The sound of the china breaking was like chalk on slate.

I was seeing this in slow motion, but it all was happening in an instant. An instant in which something held me paralyzed, to my shame. Then Elizabeth was saying, "Give me that," and taking the silver lighter. She stood, ghost-tall, the flame making skeletal hollows in her face.

"Please. Sit down and remain quiet." Uncannily everyone obeyed. Mrs. Gass was whimpering now, and somebody moaned. Not Lissa. I remembered that afterward; that my first thought was of Lissa and that I didn't hear a sound from her and could not see her.

By the light of the frail flame Elizabeth made her way into the Walnut Room, then the sitting room beyond. It was several minutes before she returned, carrying two oil lamps. One she left on the Walnut Room's library table, the other she brought with her to the dining room.

"I'm sorry to take so long. The lamps in the other rooms had gone out, and their oil was spilled. I had to refill them. Steve, would you and Paul please take care of the spill before we have a fire?" She said it perfectly naturally, but the significance of the statement escaped no one. There was another taut stillness.

"It's a manifestation. A genuine manifestation," Mr. Martin said eagerly.

"Nonsense," Mrs. Wilson said robustly. "It was a draft, like Mr. Gass said. As for the chair and plant stand—" She didn't finish, but she looked straight at Mike Riley.

"I didn't do it," he protested instantly. In the dim light his face looked green.

Draft—I bolted from my chair into the dining porch and there was Lissa, her back pressed to a narrow strip of wall between the windows. I knelt and hugged her, but it was several minutes before I could warm her enough so she could move. She drew a sobbing breath. "I'm sorry . . . I'm so sorry. . . ."

"Sorry for what?" I straightened, startled. "Lissa, you're not trying to say *you* had anything to do with this!"

She jerked in my arms and her eyes focused, as though dragged back to consciousness. "No, of course not!"

I guided her back into the other room. In my absence a low-voiced argument had been taking place. "It's a—what do you call it, honey? Like that movie we watched on TV last week." Mrs. Gass appealed to her husband.

He made an exclamation. "A *poltergeist?*"

"Poltergeist—a mischievous spirit in the house." Mr. Martin pounced on the suggestion. "Now, that's interesting!"

"The only mischievous spirits in this place don't belong to any ghosts," Martha Gibbs said firmly from the kitchen doorway. "Storm's started up again, in case you've been too busy imagining things to notice. This is an old house and it shakes when the wind blows."

Matter-of-factly she picked up the silver pitcher and set it back in place. "Miz Lancaster, you better tell the cleaning girl not to put so much polish on the sideboard next time, so this won't slide. Now, the electric lines may be down, but my gas stove's working. You folks going to eat this fancy meal I cooked for you, or aren't you?"

"Mrs. Gibbs is right," Steve said easily. He held

out Mrs. Wilson's chair, and she promptly sat down. The others, after a hesitation, sat as well.

Our lobster bisque, incredibly, was still warm enough to eat. Everything had occurred in a span of only a few minutes.

Ella cleared the soup plates and returned with the main course: a choice of beef or pollock, a fish like cod. Mrs. Gass, I noticed, had not been scared out of her appetite. She helped herself liberally. "Please," Mr. Ikawa inquired, soft-voiced, "would it not be wise to telephone the police?"

"Phone lines are down too," Ella put in. "I tried to call the electric company to see if the power'd be on in time so's we could use the dishwasher. Those dratted lines always come down when we lose tree branches!"

But I hadn't heard any branches crash. Something nagged at the corners of my mind.

Paul, having finished mopping up the spilled oil, located a flashlight and went downstairs. "The lines aren't down," he reported when he returned. "The inside line's broken off at the main box. It must have gotten damaged last week." He looked hard at Elizabeth; he meant *during the fire*. He looked from the Gasses to Mr. Martin with disfavor. "You can't blame that on ghosts. They don't have to use telephones."

"Now, that's an interesting concept—" Mr. Martin was about to start off again. Mrs. Wilson interrupted.

"Mr. Ikawa, do tell us. Do you have a tradition of ghost belief like ours in Japan?" She led him safely off onto the subject of Shinto ancestor worship. Gradually the tension around the table eased.

After dinner the proposed games and music

were forgotten. The Curtises and Wallaces took
their children off to bed, and stayed upstairs with
them. To my relief the Rileys soon followed.
Elizabeth caught my eye. "Will you look after
Lissa and Kevin, please?" I hated leaving her
downstairs to cope, but I did so. Kevin led the
way, eager to prove that he was fearless, while
Lissa clung to my hand. At the doorway of her
room she stopped.

"Can I sleep with you tonight?"

"Of course, if you want to." I took her in,
locking the door automatically behind us. How
ridiculous, locking out ghosts and poltergeists, I
thought. But there wasn't a poltergeist, was there?

Lissa went through the connecting bath to her
room. She darted back quickly, clutching her nightgown and the Cabbage Patch Kid doll that custom-
arily adorned her bed.

"Lissa," I said carefully, "why were you so frightened when the room went dark? What did you
see?"

Lissa, undressing with her back to me, stiffened.
"I didn't see anything. It was dark."

"What did you hear, then? Lissa, *tell me*. Maybe
I can help."

"You can't help. Nobody can." She turned giving
me one of those strange looks. "You don't believe
in ghosts, do you? Or poltergeists."

"I don't believe there's a poltergeist in Rockcove
Hall, that's for sure." Would she recognize the
evasion in that answer?

The air in the room suddenly shimmered and
crackled. I looked at her, standing there dumbly
submissive, and I took hold of her and shook her.
"Lissa, you *must* tell me what you know—about

anything that's happened. Can't you see it's terribly important?"

"I can't."

"You must!"

Lissa shook her head faintly. "You don't understand."

She said it with the dull certainty of despair, and it was all I could get out of her.

It was now nearly ten, but I didn't want to go back downstairs until Lissa was asleep. I sat down in the rocker by the fireplace, trying to sort things through. Had Bill left yet? It comforted me to think he was still here. The plain fact was, I had no idea whom else I could trust, and that included the members of my own family.

It was not long after that that Mrs. Gass started screaming.

Somehow, this time I wasn't scared. Maybe it was because of the comforting aura in my rooms; maybe it was because I was all scared out. I unlocked my door and flung it open as Kevin's door opened too. People were running up and down stairs. In the central corridor outside Elizabeth's old room stood Mrs. Gass, an apparition in a shocking pink lacy nightgown with red hair rollers, alternately screeching and slapping at her husband's hand as he tried to pat her. Steve and Elizabeth, Paul and Bill were all on the main staircase, but I reached her first.

"Mrs. Gass, what happened?"

She jerked her hand at the bedroom door, and I dashed in.

I understood, sooner than perhaps anyone but Kevin and Lissa and Mike could, what had happened. Somebody had shortsheeted the Gasses' bed. Someone had greased the inside door handle with strong-smelling muscle rub. Old summer camp tricks. What made them ugly was the object that reposed in the middle of the folded sheet. A dead squirrel, crusted with dried blood.

Elizabeth looked and gagged. Paul grabbed the corpse by the tail and carried it away. Mr. Riley eyed his son, who looked fascinated but not guilty. Mrs. Gass clutched her husband.

"I won't stay here! Not one more instant! Honey, I want you to get dressed and take me away from here *now!*"

"I don't know where you'll go," Steve said flatly. "It's a holiday weekend. Every room in town will be filled. If the wires are down, it wouldn't be smart to try to drive down to Gloucester."

"I won't stay in that room," Mrs. Gass insisted.

"You can take mine." Elizabeth was holding on to her calm with effort. "Steve, Paul, will you please switch our bureaus? That will be easier than moving clothes by the armload."

"No need to switch them. We'll be leaving first thing in the morning," Mr. Gass said firmly, comforting his wife. I got clean towels and linens and made up Elizabeth's new room for them.

And that was the end of that, except Bill came in to help me spread the sheets and said with decision, "I'm staying here the rest of the night. I don't care where. I can sleep on the couch downstairs."

"You can sleep in Lissa's room. She's in with me." And so he did.

The Gasses left before breakfast, and that was the beginning of a general exit. Everyone had excellent reasons, but the fact remained, they left.

I saw Elizabeth's eyes as the projected profits from the holiday weekend went down the drain. And they weren't her only worry. Ailsa showed up in the midmorning, and after hearing about the latest disaster, she voiced my secret thought.

"What do you think will happen when the news about this gets around?"

"Then it simply can't get around." Elizabeth's lips were set tight.

Ailsa gave an eloquent shrug. "With Albert Henry on the premises?"

Mr. Martin, the one person we could cheerfully have dispensed with, was cheerfully staying. So were Mrs. Wilson and Mr. Ikawa. He went around photographing all the spots where the "poltergeist" had appeared, and Mrs. Wilson, blessedly, took Kevin and Lissa downtown and treated them to all sorts of distracting and unnecessary things. Bill stayed all morning, primarily because he could not get me away from the house.

The phone company couldn't send anyone to fix the line because it was a Saturday, and Asey could not be found. Paul repaired it under Ailsa's eye. "I wish you'd try to take a nap," she told Elizabeth sternly.

Elizabeth shrugged. "I couldn't sleep."

"Then lie down anyway."

She shook her head.

At midday Bill gave up on me and left after giving me firm orders to phone him once the line was fixed. He would be at the newspaper office with his uncle. He and Ailsa left. Paul, mainly to get them where they couldn't go spreading stories, took Mr. Martin and also Mr. Ikawa for a ride around Folly Cove and Dogtown Common. Elizabeth grimly started trying to track down Asey Dawson to repaper the wall above her bed. At last she slammed into her car, shouted, "I'm going to pick up some paper and do the job myself," and gunned down the road toward Gloucester.

I was alone in Rockcove Hall and I went for a swim, letting the sunshine and solitude wash over me. There was no sense of haunting here now, only a welcome tranquility. But as I floated on my back in the pool, my mind kept going over and over the events of the past—could it only be two weeks? Something was not right, and that something was accelerating. No, not something— somethings. I knew in my bones that some of those things had logical explanations, somehow: the poltergeist, the candles and the brownouts, the break in the telephone line (I could not believe that was accidental)—yes, even the fire, however drastic. The other things—the paralysis that had gripped Lissa, her depression, her despair, above all, that crushed and bloodied squirrel—those were *sick*.

There had to be an order and a pattern somewhere. Otherwise there were simply—too many ghosts, too many unexplainable events for one summer, one family, one house. I had the uncomfortable, insistent feeling that I already had the key, and somehow couldn't see it.

Thirteen

As I floated in the water, a shadow fell across me. I looked up, behind me, and almost screamed.

A strange man in a business suit stood there, looking at me doubtfully. "Mrs. Lancaster?"

I climbed out quickly, reaching for my robe. "My cousin's not available at present. Can I help you?"

He frowned. "That's odd. I'm from CJG Developers. My secretary received a call saying that Mrs. Lancaster had reconsidered our offer and wanted to meet with me this afternoon to discuss a price."

"A—price?" Then it registered. "If you're referring to an offer to buy Rockcove Hall, she isn't interested."

"I'll wait." He sat down firmly in a deck chair.

To my relief, Paul's car pulled into the driveway at that moment, and Mr. Martin and Mr. Ikawa stepped out.

"Paul!" I shouted.

He came running. I explained things tersely, and left Paul to get rid of the man. Fortunately he succeeded before Elizabeth returned. She climbed out of the car wearily, dragging shopping bags full of wallpaper just as Martha Gibbs, who'd arrived to start dinner, emerged grimly from the house.

"Good thing you got back. Somebody, probably that brat, unplugged your new freezer and everything's got spoilt. The pantry floor's a flood, and what'll we do for dinner?"

Elizabeth broke down. The shopping bags dropped from her hands and she stared at Martha blankly. Suddenly, shockingly, she stamped both feet and burst into tears. "*No more!* I have had—every single thing—that I can take!"

Mrs. Gibbs went straight to her and gathered Elizabeth in her arms. "Phone Mr. McGovern and that Miss Craig," she ordered me, leading Elizabeth inside.

I couldn't reach Steve, but Ailsa was there within ten minutes and announced she had summoned Elizabeth's family doctor. "You certainly are going to see him. After I twisted his arm to make a house call?" she said firmly when Elizabeth protested.

She succeeded in making Elizabeth lie down, and after the doctor left, she herself drove into town to have the prescriptions filled. She also brought back fresh groceries for dinner. Paul and I cleaned the kitchen, and it was terrible. Paul was in one of his silent, sullen moods, remarking merely that all that happened showed that starting a hotel was a bad idea.

"Who could predict an electric plug would get pulled out?" I replied with spirit.

Paul just looked at me. "What do you think caused it? Ghosts?"

Privately my suspicions rested on the now departed Mike Riley.

Dinner was quiet. Elizabeth was still lying down, sedated. There were only the three guests now. Mrs. Wilson dined alone cheerfully with a book; Mr. Martin and Mr. Ikawa joined forces at a shared table, and to my dismay I could overhear Mr. Martin rattling away importantly about psychic phenomena.

There was no poltergeist activity that evening, but during dinner I was called away to the telephone three times. The first two were reservation cancellations, with no reason given. (Some guests, probably the Gasses, must have been talking since their departure, I thought, my heart sinking.) The third time the phone rang I answered, and there was—nothing. No voice, no dead line, not even heavy breathing. Just a live stillness that continued as I kept saying "Hello?" with rising intensity. I finally hung up.

I had difficulty sleeping that night, and I was not the only one. The house creaked. I thought I heard footsteps coming up the stairs, but when I bolted from the bed to unlock the door and look out, I found no one there. I went into Lissa's room and found her, hugging her knees, in the window seat looking toward the sea. She did not stir at my entrance. When I asked her if she wanted to come to my room, she pulled herself back to consciousness with an effort and shook her head.

"Lissa, are you all right?"

"Why wouldn't I be?"

I looked at her, perplexed. Then the ceiling creaked above our heads, and we both looked up.

"Wind again. At least we know that isn't somebody creeping around," I said lightly. "There are no rooms above us." I produced a laugh. "And ghosts don't make footsteps!"

Lissa flicked me a pitying glance. "Yes, they do."

Before I could ask her to explain that, something crashed. Not above us, but somewhere around the corner. In Elizabeth's room . . .

I dashed out as I heard Elizabeth's gasp. Mr. Ikawa emerged from his room in royal blue silk pajamas, and together we converged on the master suite. I thanked God that the electricity was not browned out; the hall chandelier responded instantly when I touched the switch.

Elizabeth's door was locked and bolted, and only her gasping breath responded to our pounding. "She has an extra set of keys in her purse," Lissa stated, and I said, "Get them," but it was Kevin who ran unquestioningly down to the darkened kitchen. He came back with the purse. I fumbled for the keys; Paul appeared, snatched the bag roughly, and produced them.

The ceiling light fixture burned in the big bedroom, glaring mercilessly on the water-stained wallpaper and on Elizabeth's haggard face. She stood rigid in the center of the room, hugging herself, staring at the heavy picture frame that had fallen from its hook behind the bed. Shards of wood and glass were scattered on the bed.

How had it missed striking Elizabeth? My eyes darted feverishly; I saw the pillows and afghan trailing from the chair and ottoman. Some reason, some thing, had kept Elizabeth that night from the bed she used to share with Dan, and that was what had saved her.

"I'm all right," Elizabeth said with effort. "It

was ridiculous of me... to react like this. I was just... startled. The plaster in this house is—is starting to crumble. That's what made the picture fall. Or else the wind."

But there was no wind. I realized that when I was back in my own bed, staring out at the trees silhouetted against the faint moonlight. Though my ears insisted on hearing a faint whistling, the branches did not move.

In the silvery reflection of my mirror shadows moved and formed, taking on a shape similar to what had been on the TV screen. Again I felt a presence. And again I knew it intended me no harm. It was somehow trying to protect me. And it was deeply troubled.

I did not doubt any of this for a moment, but there was no part of it that I could prove.

I didn't think that I would sleep, but I must have. I awoke around nine to a pounding on my door. *Elizabeth,* was my first thought. But when I unlocked and opened the door, Paul strode in and flung a newspaper on the little sofa.

"Some friend you've got! Or did you tell him it would be all right to do this?"

The Gloucester newspaper, Bill's uncle's newspaper, carried the story of Rockcove Hall's ghosts, past and present. The story was plastered over half of the front page.

"What did Elizabeth say?" I asked through dry lips.

"Elizabeth hasn't seen it. She isn't up. Do you have any idea what you've done to us?" Paul demanded.

"It wasn't my fault!"

"You brought that creep here! When you knew

he was working for a newspaper! He was hanging around almost every time something happened, thanks to you. Heaven knows how he's managing to hold his job. And I thought you were supposed to be here for work!"

I stared at him. Then something burst. *"You're jealous!* That's the only reason—"

For an instant I thought Paul would deny it. Then he flung himself out. I stood there, shaking. Then I pulled myself together, took a shower, and ran downstairs.

Elizabeth was still absent, but our three guests were reading the newspapers avidly. Then the phone started ringing. Ailsa, then Steve. Two more cancellations of reservations. Then, unexpectedly, four calls asking to book rooms—in two cases, for a week or more. In between those calls the phone rang twice, but no one was there when I reached it.

"What was that?" Elizabeth asked, coming downstairs as I hung up after the second one.

"Must have been a wrong number. They hung up after I said Rockcove Hall. Elizabeth—"

"Don't worry. Martha Gibbs brought me up the paper. I know it wasn't your fault. We'll probably start getting calls from kids pretending to be ghosts," Elizabeth said, reaching for the phone as it rang again. "What? No, we are *not* interested in selling. And don't call again!"

"The real estate company? CJG?" I asked. She nodded. "Elizabeth, you don't think perhaps—"

"No, I do *not*. Don't even suggest the possibility again. I get enough of that kind of advice from Ailsa!" Elizabeth's voice was tight.

"You didn't sleep, did you?" I asked gently. She shook her head.

"My nerves feel like a violin string that's been wound too tight. I need a cup of coffee, then I'll be all right."

Twice that day I put my hand on the telephone to call Bill Rhodes. It was teatime before I could make myself do it, and there was no answer.

I thanked God for one thing at least—that the guests we had were not the type who'd panic. Mr. Martin, for all his fascination with ghosts, was not afraid of them. Mr. Ikawa displayed a scientific interest. Mrs. Wilson was the kind of wise woman who'd seen so much that little could upset her. She was a godsend where Elizabeth and the children were concerned. Kevin's fearlessness was wearing thin, and when Deborah started whimpering during dinner, he looked frankly scared.

"Oh, Kevin, you know how dogs love to carry on about nothing," Mrs. Wilson said. She glanced, as we all did, at the windows toward which Deborah was pointing. I felt the skin crawl on my neck.

In the wan moonlight something moved out on the point of rocks. Something in soft shimmering copper; while we watched, it drifted toward the cove.

As suddenly as it had appeared, it was gone.

Deborah's keening rose, then abruptly stopped.

Fourteen

Monday began badly. Mr. Ikawa came downstairs very early and found me in the kitchen starting the coffee urns before Mrs. Gibbs's arrival. He bowed politely.

"Oh, Mr. Ikawa... I'm sorry, breakfast won't be ready for another hour. Can I make you tea or coffee?"

He gave that formal little head bow again. "Excuse me, please. I wished to speak to a member of the family before the servants are here. You have time, please?"

So he knew I was a relative. I wondered who had told him that. It was no secret, but Elizabeth and I had agreed it would look less than professional to broadcast it. "Yes, of course. Is anything wrong?" What I meant was, did he plan to check out too?

"No, not wrong." He glanced around, then led the way into the Walnut Room, where we could see if anyone approached. "I wish to ask about the family ghost. Mr. Martin and your workman, Dawson, have said much—"

"They're just tall stories," I said hastily.

"Please. I am a scientist, not a storyteller. But I wish to know whether there is a legend connected to Rockcove Hall about a boat without a captain. I think I should inform you I saw such a boat circling around the cove last night."

He said it so calmly. The skin on my neck began to crawl. "What do you think you saw?" I asked carefully.

"Excuse me. As I said, I am a scientist. I also am accustomed to sleeping very lightly. After the excitement of the past weekend, I awoke sometime after three. I wished to examine the point of rocks where the apparition of the captain's lady seemed to appear. An interesting illusion, but undoubtedly a trick of light or perhaps reflection. I hoped to discover what had caused it, so I let myself out through the terrace doorway and strolled across the lawn. As I was coming back from the point, I saw a small powerboat pull into the dock, then away again. There was no one at the wheel."

My pulses throbbed. "You can't be sure of that," I said with dry lips.

"Oh, yes," he answered calmly. "The moonlight was faint, but there was enough to see." He produced the by now familiar camera. "I also had this with me. It is a model from my company with special film that I am testing. It will take photographs without a flash in almost no light. I had hoped, if the ghost phenomenon occurred again, to photograph it. I did photograph the speedboat more than once. Considering the other happenings at Rockcove Hall, I felt I should report this to the owners. Mrs. Lancaster is the proper person, of course. However—" He paused delicately.

He was thinking about the condition Elizabeth had been in yesterday. "I'm very grateful," I said, and meant it. "I will see that the situation is looked into. I would appreciate it if you wouldn't share this with anyone, and—would you possibly give me your roll of film? I'll have it developed somewhere trustworthy and return the prints to you."

"Yes, of course." Mr. Ikawa rewound the film cartridge, opened the camera, and handed the film to me. "I also found this out on the point."

It was a small worn handkerchief, lace-edged, embroidered with the letter *L*. "No doubt it was left by an earlier visitor. Do not be alarmed, Miss Clayborne. In my experience, all such phenomena as we have witnessed eventually prove to have logical explanations. As I said, I am a scientist, not a storyteller."

Thank God for that, I thought humbly. And thank God it was he, not Mr. Martin, who had decided to take a predawn stroll.

The story of the boat bothered me all through breakfast. Of course it couldn't really have been unmanned, but why was it in our harbor? A curiosity-seeker? A fisherman, poaching on Rockcove Hall fishing rights? That would explain why there had been no lights.

It wasn't till I was bullying Lissa through a plate of scrambled eggs that the forgotten thing nagging at my memory suddenly became clear. A ghost boat. Asey had claimed to have seen a ghost boat cut in front of the *Sea Witch* the night Dan died. I would pump Asey on that story today, I resolved, and as soon as morning chores were over, I would explore the dock. Alone. I put my bathing suit on under my T-shirt just in case I got wet.

But no phone calls could turn up Asey's whereabouts. He had not been at his rooming house for two nights. And I didn't get to visit the dock because I was interrupted by a reporter who showed up on our doorstep right after breakfast. He was from a Boston paper, and he wanted a bright, cheery human interest story about Rockcove Hall and its ghost infestation.

As soon as Mrs. Wilson heard the man identify himself, she pounced on Mr. Martin and dragged him off to explore the point with her. I got rid of the reporter, then sent Lissa up to check on Elizabeth, who was still sleeping, and I answered the telephone. One cancellation, three reservations, one call from the real estate development company, and one somebody-there-not-breathing.

"What was that?" Paul demanded, stalking in as I shouted, "I know you're there!"

I dumped the receiver down. "Kids playing games again. This is the third or fourth time it's happened."

"We'll probably be getting ghost moans next," Paul said disgustedly. He shot me a look. "Heard from that dirty journalist of yours yet?"

"He's not dirty, and he's not mine—" I broke off as the doorbell rang.

It was a reporter from a Boston TV station, complete with mobile camera crew. I thanked my lucky stars Elizabeth was not yet down, and Mr. Martin was not around. "No, you cannot bring the camera in. No comment. The owner is not available at present and does not wish to make a statement."

"Is it true that there is a history of unsolved deaths in connection with Rockcove Hall? Are you a spokesman for the Lancaster family? Is there any connection between the recent fire and the poltergeist activity and the violent death of Daniel Lancaster?"

"It was *not* a violent death! Not the way you mean. Oh, please—" I was losing control of myself, and I knew it. Just then, like a blessing or a curse, a figure materialized behind the camera crew. A figure I had all too much reason to know was flesh and blood. Bill Rhodes, in a sport shirt and jeans, a puzzled and then comprehending expression on his face.

The TV crew didn't see him. Paul did. Paul, coming around the corner of the house and stopping dead, took one look at Bill and charged through the group of network people, his fists swinging. The camera swung around. So did the microphone. Bill, taken off balance at first, came back immediately, also swinging.

I did the only thing I could think of—pulled off the T-shirt I was wearing over my bathing suit and threw it over the camera lens. "Get inside!" I ordered the combatants sharply. Miraculously they obeyed. The three of us flung ourselves into the hall and slammed the door. Paul snapped the locks shut. Ella Hazen was standing with a dustcloth in the sitting room and I shouted, "Lock up! Quick!" and she jumped to it, with the help of Mrs. Wilson and Mr. Ikawa. Where Mr. Martin was, I didn't have time yet to worry over.

I dragged Bill and Paul upstairs to my own sitting room and locked the door. "Are you out of your minds? The last thing we need is to settle that newspaper story on TV!"

"I can't blame Lancaster," Bill said, rubbing the bruised spot on his jaw, "but I had nothing to do with that story. I came over here to tell you so."

"You liar," Paul nearly shouted.

"I swear it, and I can prove it." Bill was looking straight at me. "Cindy, *think!* The poltergeist activity took place Friday night, and I stayed here till early afternoon Saturday! The Sunday edition of the paper was being printed before then! Call any newspaper and ask if you don't believe me."

"But all that background material, about the hall and the captain's lady and Dan's death."

"All right, I admit I was digging into that. In the newspaper morgue, where anyone could find it! I was curious, and you know why." Yes, I did. I lowered my eyelids. "One of the paper's staff reporters was in Rockport Saturday morning when Martin started blabbing about what had happened at dinner. He went straight to my uncle with the story."

"After he pumped Asey," I said through stiff lips.

"Yes, after he pumped Asey. If it's any comfort, the reason that interview's 'to be continued' is because at that point Dawson passed out cold. The reporter hasn't been able to find him since. And you two might also like to know," Bill said distinctly, "that my uncle really chewed me out for not bringing the story in myself. Asked me what kind of reporter I thought I could be if I let personal considerations get in the way of objectivity."

"Some objectivity!" Paul jeered.

"Shut up," I said absently. "That's the trouble

with all of us. We're too close to what's happening. What we need is some hard facts."

A current of air ran down my neck. I stiffened, noting that Paul and Bill had not reacted.

Like a sleepwalker I unlocked the door and moved out into the corridor, around the corner, and up the stairs to the third floor as the others followed.

The third-floor hall was still. The doors of the three unrented rooms were locked; so was Mr. Martin's, and he did not answer when I knocked. Bill took a step toward me, and Paul held him back. "What is it?" Paul asked intently.

I shook my head. "I don't know, I—I thought I heard something."

The current of air moved again down my neck. I turned in the direction from which it had come.

The door to the attic was ajar, its lock still turned and keyless though the bolt was shot.

Paul gave a muttered exclamation and sprang forward. "No," I said. "No." I went to the door, opened it wide, and started up the stairs.

Paul tried to follow. Bill grabbed him. "Didn't you hear her?"

"Don't you know it could be dangerous—"

We all three froze. Footsteps, unmistakably Albert Henry Martin's, were coming up from the second floor. In one swift movement Bill closed the door to the attic stairs and stood against it. Paul moved off to intercept Mr. Martin. I climbed, as if predestined, to the attic.

The slant-roofed space was still and bright with sunlight. Everything stood as it had been left on Friday, including the little chest. Only one thing was changed. Another, smaller door stood open on narrow, twisting stairs. The stairs to the widow's walk...

I moved up them, and my guardian presence moved with me. Up onto the small rectangle of space on which generations of sailors' wives had paced and waited. The Chippendale-style railing rose, hip-high. Beyond, below, all of Cape Ann spread like a toy world. I stood there dizzily, gazing, and the air was intoxicatingly thin. Something pulled me toward the railing; something else held me back.

I forced myself to turn back to the trapdoor and the stairs, and then I saw it. In the far corner, gleaming in the sun: a small, pink-tinged glass sphere.

I picked it up and put it in my pocket, and when I was back downstairs with Bill and Paul, I did not speak of it at all.

Fifteen

Bill got rid of Mr. Martin by arranging to take him into town and interview him on his artwork. Whether the paper would print any of it, I neither knew nor cared. I went straight to Elizabeth's room and knocked on the door. There was no answer, and the door was locked. I went down to the kitchen, with Paul on my heels.

"She hasn't come down," Martha said flatly. "I know that for sure because I've been laying for her to talk about tonight's dinner. We got two more guests arriving. Everybody's gone out, including your beau."

"What happened to the TV people?" I asked apprehensively.

"I got rid of 'em," Martha said succinctly. "And I locked all the doors in case they come sneaking round again. Miss Craig come by, and she's taken the children to her place to spend the day. I wouldn't let her wake Miz Lancaster, on account of she needs her sleep, but don't you think we better disturb her now? The morning's 'most gone."

Elizabeth's purse was on the kitchen table. I

helped myself to her keys, making a mental note to ask her to give me a duplicate set.

An electric light burned in the master bedroom despite the fact it was midmorning. Elizabeth was sleeping heavily, her hair and nightgown clinging damply to her skin.

"Make her sit up," Paul ordered, and disappeared into the bathroom. He returned with a wet washcloth. "Squeeze it on her if you have to. She must have taken something to knock her out."

Elizabeth came struggling up from the depths of sleep. "Why, what—" She looked at us bending over her, and her eyes focused with difficulty. "What's wrong?"

"It's ten minutes to noon. We were worried," Paul said sardonically. "You managed to miss a lot of excitement."

"*What?*" Elizabeth sat straight up. Then she put her hand to her forehead with a groan. "Get me some coffee, will you, Paul? Make it black. I was awake most of the night and by four A.M. I was so loopy, I dug out the sleeping pills the doctor prescribed for me." She shot a glance at the bedside table with a grimace. "Tell me what's happened."

"We've landed in the big time. A TV station sent a camera crew as a result of that newspaper story, that's all." Time enough to tell her about the attic when she was more awake. I shot Paul a look. "Get that coffee, will you? Bring some Danish too."

Paul stood a minute, irresolute, but then he went. I told Elizabeth about the scene outside, trying to make light of it. I told her, too, that Bill had cleared himself of guilt in the matter of the newspaper story. "And Asey appears to be off on a toot somewhere, so they may not get that follow-up interview with him after all."

"Let's hope not," Elizabeth said prayerfully.

"At least the whole thing doesn't seem to be hurting business." I told her about the additional reservations.

"Probably the kind of people who rubberneck at traffic accidents," Elizabeth said grimly. "Well, at least it's money. Don't accept any reservations from families with young children. Adults only. I've made up my mind."

Paul returned with the breakfast items. I took them from him at the door, then shut it. I stayed with Elizabeth while she showered, gulped down the pills her doctor had prescribed, and pulled on a denim shirtdress. Her fingers fumbled with the buttons. She dropped an earring and stood looking down at it dumbly. I retrieved it.

"Sorry. My fingers don't seem to be working right. . . . *Oh!*" The earring spun out of her hand again. She pulled the other out, too, and slammed it on the bureau. "I just can't bother with stuff like this."

"Mrs. Gibbs is waiting for you." I steered her down and left her with the cook. When I left the kitchen, Paul cornered me.

"Did you tell her about the attic?"

"Not yet."

"I want to talk to you." Paul literally marched me up to my rooms and shut the door behind us. "Don't set yourself up to be Elizabeth's keeper the way you've done with Lissa."

"That's a rotten thing to say! Lissa needs a friend who understands her. And Elizabeth certainly doesn't need a keeper."

"Elizabeth," Paul said flatly, "is cracking up. You'd know it if you weren't being so deliberately blind."

"She has a lot on her mind. We don't need to add this business with the attic to it. If you and I make a point of checking the dead bolt regularly—"

"If Elizabeth is going to operate this place as a hotel, *she* has to take the responsibility. *She* owns the business. *She* owns Rockcove Hall now."

"And you think she should pack up her knitting and turn the whole place over to you. We know!" I was picking a fight again. I couldn't help myself.

"All right!" Paul swung around to me, his face close to mine. "All right, I love this place. I admit it. And I'm not just thinking about myself; I'm thinking about her and the kids. We could lose the hall completely if some curious guest goes poking around the widow's walk and falls! Everyone warned Elizabeth she was getting in over her head starting a hotel, but would she listen? If she can't even remember to keep that door locked—"

"How do you know she didn't? Her keys were right in the kitchen, where anyone could get them!"

We both stopped short as the magnitude of the implication sunk in.

"It still holds," Paul insisted. "If she's so ditzy she doesn't have the sense to put them where they're safe—"

"Elizabeth is the least ditzy person I know!"

"Cindy, wake up! You saw how she was when the freezer broke. You saw her the other night when the picture fell. She can't take the pressure."

"Anybody'd crack a little under what's been happening!"

"I haven't," Paul said doggedly, overlooking the fight he'd picked with Bill. "I know you idolize the woman, but face facts! She's not a businessperson, she's an artist. She's probably still whacked up from my brother's death. How do you think she's going to handle it if—"

"If what?"

He didn't finish. He took ahold of me by the arms and just stood there staring into my face, only a few inches away from his.

"You're hurting me."

He let go of me then and swung away, thrusting his fists into his pockets.

"If what?" I prompted.

"It doesn't matter."

"Yes, it does. How do I think Elizabeth is going to handle it if what happens? What do you think is apt to happen next, Paul? Or do you already know?"

I swear to God, I didn't know where that last question came from. I put out my hand to catch it back, but it was too late.

"*I'm* not the ghost of Rockcove Hall," Paul said. "You can accept that or reject it, I don't care. What I do care about is what will happen if—"

He stopped.

"What will happen if we don't find out who the ghost is," I finished. "I suppose I should say the poltergeist."

Paul looked away from me, then back. When he spoke, it was in an entirely different voice. "I mean what it will do to us when we do."

I knew exactly what Paul was about to say, and why, and I could not stop him.

"Hasn't it occurred to you," Paul asked with

rough compassion, "that there's one person who exactly fits the specifications for a poltergeist? And that's Lissa."

"No!"

"I may be a mere beach bum, not a smartass reporter," Paul said sarcastically, "but I have had one year of college. I took Psych 101. Means, motive, opportunity. Lissa's the right age. She's been in shock ever since Dan was killed; she's got a thing about the Watcher; she's living in a dream world. She can't bear the way her world's changed, and that includes paying guests, and a working mother with a boyfriend in the wings. You tell *me* if a hypersensitive, overimaginative preadolescent female couldn't or wouldn't produce a poltergeist to drive the intruders away!"

"I don't believe it," I said doggedly. But it was my eyes that faltered.

"Grow up," Paul said in a tone that was a mixture of tenderness and anger. Then he left the room.

I stood staring at the mirror that hung on the wall between Lissa's room and mine. There was nothing reflected in it but my own face, with a curious drowned look on it. After several minutes I went downstairs, looked up the number of the newspaper in Gloucester, called it, and I asked for Bill.

"What's happened?" he asked immediately when he heard my voice.

"Nothing. I just need to get away from here. Would you feel like taking me for a late lunch?"

"You got it."

He must have broken the speed limit getting to the hall. "I stopped at a deli and picked up a

picnic. Better than going to a restaurant and being
recognized." He drove inland to Dogtown Common and parked the car, and we walked through
the wild undergrowth and sat on a stone wall that
was all that remained from an early colonist's
house.

I had wanted to escape from Rockcove Hall and
all that haunted it. I should have known that was
impossible. Within fifteen minutes Bill had gotten
everything that had happened since his departure
out of me.

"You won't want to hear it, but everything
Lancaster said was true. About the psychological
profile of the typical poltergeist," Bill said. Then
his face softened. "Don't look so afraid. Lissa's not
the only likely candidate."

"What do you mean?"

"Well, you know I've been doing some digging
in the newspaper morgue," Bill said. "I read up on
your brother-in-law's accident. It does sound as if
any police investigation was cut off."

"Maybe the newspaper just didn't get all the
facts."

"The newspaper gets a look at all the police
blotters on the cape. There was an autopsy; there
always is in cases of unexpected death. The coroner ruled accidental death by drowning. The question is why there was a boat accident at all."

"There was a storm, and there was mist or fog.
He took the boat because the road was closed."

"Cindy," Bill said, "there's no record of the road
being closed to drivers. By a fallen branch, or for
any other reason."

I just looked at him. "I don't believe it! Wouldn't

the police have investigated the death more thoroughly, knowing that somebody lied to him?"

"Not necessarily. He could have lied to his wife about it—or she could have lied herself."

"She wouldn't. She had no reason to."

"I agree with you. But somebody wants to stop Rockcove Hall from being used as a hotel. Or get her out of there. Or both." I stirred uneasily, and Bill saw it. "What bell did that just ring?" he asked.

"*Ring* is the right word." I told him about the nobody-there phone calls I'd been getting, and he frowned.

"I don't like that. That's sick."

"So's a poltergeist, and a ghost boat, and all the rest. And I don't believe Lissa and Elizabeth are"—what was the phrase Paul had used?—"whacked up!"

"Somebody wouldn't have to be mentally disturbed, or even a trifle paranoid, to stage all this. It could be based on good old rational motives, like revenge or greed. Dan Lancaster lost a lot of money in investments, didn't he? I haven't been poking; that was hinted at in the newspaper story. Probably part of Asey Dawson's contribution. Or local gossip. From what you've told me, Dan was no fool, so why did he lose so much? Why is that real estate development company so eager to buy the hall, and what would be different if Dan were still alive?"

I stared. "You're suggesting Dan was—*murdered?*"

"I'm only putting in words what you've been thinking," Bill said patiently. "I'll give you something else that maybe you haven't thought of yet. What happens to the hall if the hotel does fail and

Elizabeth does freak out? Lissa's not the only family member who has a large psychological and emotional stake in the place. And maybe something more tangible too."

"You mean *Paul?*"

"I mean only that he has his own ax to grind where Rockcove Hall's concerned. You can't know for sure that you can trust him."

"I don't know *whom* I can trust!" I wailed, and to my intense annoyance burst into tears.

"You can trust me. I don't have any ax to grind. At least not where Rockcove Hall is concerned," Bill said with significance, and took me in his arms.

We lay on the rocks in the warm sun, and what followed should have been thoroughly distracting and mood-lifting. Except it wasn't. And finally Bill drove me back home to Rockcove Hall.

Sixteen

It looked so serene with its white paint and red geraniums sparkling in the sun. Like a fairy-tale castle imprisoned by a spell. No sign of life moved anywhere. Tonight's new guests had not yet arrived, and the shades were drawn. The doors were probably locked too. I fished in my purse for the keys before getting out of the car, and my fingers encountered Mr. Ikawa's rolls of film.

"What is it?" Bill asked, watching me.

"Pictures of a ghost. Maybe. Do you know anywhere you could get these developed while you wait? And *not* for newspaper publication!"

"Trust me," Bill said, and took them, and drove off.

Trust—how I was beginning to dread that word.

I went inside, where the hall waited to receive its guests. Deborah slumbered in a patch of sunlight on the terrace. Paul and the *Sea Witch* both were gone. In the kitchen Martha and Ella talked cheerfully over dinner preparations. Kevin and Lissa were out with Ailsa, and Elizabeth was setting bouquets out on the dining tables.

"That's my job," I exclaimed contritely.

"It's all right. You need a break, and I need something to keep me occupied." Elizabeth ran both hands through her hair. "I feel as if I'm jumping out of my skin."

"Maybe you should take a nap."

"I can't sleep. I tried." She laughed shakily. "This isn't me. I feel as if I'm standing off watching someone else in a bad movie."

I went upstairs. It was too early yet to dress for dinner. Where were Mr. Ikawa and Mr. Martin, and what was the artist up to? Had that reporter caught up with Asey yet? Mrs. Wilson would be leaving in another day or so, and I would miss her. The thoughts flitted across my mind's eye like shimmering bits of glass.

What was Lissa doing?

Lissa could be the poltergeist.

I could not, would not, believe it.

I had seen Lissa, held her, on the dining porch right after the poltergeist activity. She had been rigid, almost catatonic. There was no way she could have been "witching" things in the other room.

Was there?

Elizabeth felt as though she were jumping out of her skin? So did I. I stared at myself in the bureau mirror. Only my own face, wide-eyed and dazed, looked back at me.

On the lace bureau runner the two iridescent glass spheres rested where I had left them, side by side. Had *Lissa* been playing on the widow's walk and left one there? Or had she put it there deliberately, for me to find? And if so, why?

I crossed restlessly to the window and looked

out toward the sea. The water sparkled, the minerals in the gray-gold rocks shimmered.

I ran downstairs and out onto the lawn, not knowing quite what possessed me. Butterflies hovered over the phlox and lupine, and bees buzzed lazily. The sparkling blue water of the swimming pool beckoned invitingly. Sailboats dotted the bay. Beyond the terrace the copper of the carriage house weather vane gave off glints.

The door to the carriage house was locked in proper order. I peered through the windows, and inside all was as I had seen it that time before—spacious, empty, clean. Not so much as a glass sphere on the floor. Yet all at once the sense of presence was back with me. Calling me, trying to hurry me, not into the carriage house but beyond it, toward the shore.

I left the carriage house and walked down to the shoreline, and every step of the way the presence went beside me. Low cliffs of rock, some two or three feet high, rimmed the entire water's edge. The rocks were sharp. That was why I'd never walked down here except to cross the wooden causeway to the little dock.

Picking my way cautiously, grateful for the rubber soles on my sandals, I groped my way along every inch of shoreline. I was uncertain; the presence with me was uncertain. She wanted to show me something urgently, and it was as if she had expected it to be out on the point. But it was not. Nothing was there except the tawny reeds swimming in the current, and the gulls, and sea spray. The spray glittered, and the light seemed to change. And my feet, at some instinctive prompting, moved back along the shore, past the dock and beyond.

The *Sea Witch* was at her mooring pole again. Paul was coming in on the outboard, and he hailed me. I did not respond. I was vaguely aware that back at the hall cars were pulling into the parking lot. But I kept on.

I was not searching for anything in particular. Something simply told me to do so, and I obeyed. Something propelled me, led me, dragged me, over the higher rocks and down again into a smaller cove invisible from the hall. And there, lying in a crevice in the rocks, I saw a heap of old rags.

Only it wasn't a heap of old rags. It was the missing Asey Dawson, found.

Seventeen

There was a bottle in his hand. It had once contained vodka but it now contained seawater that flowed in and out, in and out, with the shifting currents. Brackish, rusty water, with little bits of algae floating in it. I saw that, and the look of the old man's drowned face, clearly, sharply, even as I was screaming and then running.

Running over the jagged, treacherous rocks. Running despite the slash the rocks made in my foot, the burn they caused on my leg when I tripped and fell, picked myself up again, and kept on running. Running straight into Paul's arms despite the proximity of Bill and a paying guest, who'd both just arrived and had come hurriedly at my screams.

"What?" Paul demanded, holding me tight as I gasped for breath.

"*Asey—*" I could only point. He let go of me and was off at a run down toward the shoreline. Bill and the new male guest were already clambering across the rocks. Then Elizabeth was there, gripping my arms, her face chalk-white.

"What happened? Not the children—"

"It's Asey Dawson. He's dead. Drowned." I was shaking. Elizabeth was rigid.

"We must call the police," she said in a shell-shocked voice. But she could not move. It was I who moved up to the house mechanically and called the police. When I emerged, Asey's body was lying on the lower lawn and Paul was working over it frantically.

"It's no use," Bill said, gruffly compassionate.

"You go to hell," Paul retorted between puffs of breath.

I crept over to take Elizabeth's hand. She seemed not to notice. We could have all been frozen into a time warp—Elizabeth and I; Bill; at a slight distance, the kitchen staff and guests—all of us focused on the two figures caught in a drama of life and death.

Then the stillness broke with a raucous shock. A siren shrilled. A police car roared into the driveway, followed by Ailsa's car. She and the children jumped out. "What's wrong?" Ailsa asked, her face white.

"It's Asey. He's dead," Elizabeth told her gently.

Before anyone could stop them, Kevin and Lissa were running down the lawn.

Kevin went straight toward Paul and Asey. I broke loose from my paralysis and stopped him. Lissa checked herself in midflight, as if she had reached the edge of an abyss. Two policemen came hurrying, and after them an ambulance corpsman with a paramedic kit. "It's no use," Lissa said in a trancelike voice. "He's dead."

I released Kevin and ran to Lissa. "Hush. We

can't know that." I knew with a sinking feeling she didn't even hear me.

"The kid's right," the corpsman said. One of the policemen pulled Paul away. The other spread a covering over the rag-doll figure, and the two corpsmen lifted it to a waiting stretcher.

Ailsa had her arms around Elizabeth. Elizabeth's eyes were closed. Ailsa's stared at the sea in shock.

Another car raced into the drive—Steve's. He came running down the slope, straight to Elizabeth.

"I heard on the shortwave radio. Elizabeth, listen to me. I'm not letting you and the children stay here any longer. It isn't safe." She didn't respond, and he took his hand and lifted her chin so she would meet his eyes. "Elizabeth, God knows this is lousy timing. I wasn't going to say anything yet. I know you're still mourning Dan, but I also know—" He controlled himself with effort. "You know I love you. I want you to marry me and let me get you out of this. Now. Somewhere safe."

"No."

It was Lissa who said that. Elizabeth just made a vague gesture, as if waving off a fly. She moved out of Steve's grasp, away from all of us, up to the house. The policemen followed.

Ailsa signaled to the kitchen staff, collected the guests, and took them all inside, presumably where Elizabeth and the police were not. I stood on the lawn watching the ambulance take away Asey's body.

Bill touched my arm. "I'd better go. I came to give you something but it can wait." I nodded and walked him to his car.

When we reached it, he just stood looking at me. "I guess one thing's come clear for you," he said at last. "Whether you trust Lancaster." I couldn't answer, and after a moment he leaned down and kissed me gently on the cheek.

After Bill drove away, I went back inside, where life had taken on the aspect of a TV show. Somebody had ushered the guests to the dining porch, where Ella Hazen and a girl from the village were serving them predinner lemonade and nibbles. Steve McGovern was with them, playing host easily. *As though Elizabeth had already accepted him, and he belonged here*—the thought flashed into my mind unavoidably.

Ailsa, according to Martha Gibbs, had taken the children up to Kevin's room and was making sure they stayed there. In the sitting room, with the door shut, Elizabeth and Paul—and then I—were questioned by the police detective. Martha hadn't been asked to join us, but she came anyway, and forced the three of us to drink scalding tea as black as ink.

The questions went on and on. When had we last seen Asey Dawson? When had we talked to him? We'd been calling around town asking for him—why? It was Paul who explained. Elizabeth was drugged with shock. Then the detective started on me. What had possessed me to go exploring on the rocks this afternoon?

Possessed me—when the detective used the term, I began to laugh. I laughed and laughed, and could not stop.

"Oh, for heaven's sake, let us alone!" Elizabeth shouted suddenly. "Haven't we been through enough?"

"What does that mean, Mrs. Lancaster?" the detective asked sharply.

"You know perfectly well what, Ben Simpson," Mrs. Gibbs retorted. "You were out here when Mr. Lancaster's body turned up, weren't you? And you read the Sunday papers! If you're asking if there's anything more than what's appeared there, no, there ain't! And there's no connection between Dan Lancaster's boating accident and an old drunk passing out on the Lancasters' shoreline and drowning himself either!"

"I didn't suggest there was, did I?" Detective Simpson put away his pen and notebook and rose to leave. I stayed put. I stayed silent. The sense of presence in the room had become such a tangible entity for me that the air was humming.

Then the three of us—Elizabeth, Paul, and I—were alone together. Elizabeth came out of her daze with a visible jolt. "Cindy, why *did* you go down there?"

"I don't know. I just knew I had to. But I didn't know it was Asey I would find."

Elizabeth seemed not to hear me. She gave an odd little shake of her head, murmured "I must dress for dinner," and left with the jerky walk of a robot.

Paul faced me, and the thrumming in the room grew stronger. "Tell me the rest of it," he ordered.

"Don't tell me what to do."

We were automatically reacting in our usual patterns, but there was no life in our antagonism. With a slight shock I realized that my animosity toward Paul had completely faded. If it hadn't, I wouldn't have run to him so automatically after I found Asey. It was as though the things we'd been through together had blotted out all the differences between us that had once seemed important.

As if he'd read my mind, Paul turned to me and took me in his arms. We clung together for a long, long time. When at last we broke away, both of us were shaking.

"Like McGovern said, the timing's lousy.... That's got to wait," Paul said. "Right now I need to know exactly what happened... what you saw before I got there. Whether you moved anything. Why you went there. It's important."

I didn't question his right to ask. "I didn't move anything. There wasn't time. You saw what I saw. Why"—I gulped for air—"I honestly don't know. Something *made* me."

"The Watcher? Or was there somebody flesh and blood hanging around? I'm not being sarcastic. It does matter."

"It wasn't anyone human. *Or* anything diabolical. Nobody was hanging around pretending to be a ghost, if that's what you mean. There was just...a presence. And it wasn't malevolent. I'd stake my life on that."

"You may have to." Paul's voice was harsh.

My mouth felt dry. "What do you mean?"

"Asey was murdered," Paul said evenly. "He was murdered just the same as my brother was. And the police aren't going to do a damn thing about it. They've already made up their minds both deaths were accidental. I know better. And you do, too, don't you?"

Eighteen

The room seemed to be whirling on an axis. "What made you decide that all of a sudden?" I whispered.

"It isn't sudden." Paul threw himself on the chintz sofa and leaned forward, his hands locked together. "I've never believed Dan's death was an accident. *Him?* He grew up here on the *Sea Witch*. I didn't believe it when Ailsa phoned me at college to tell me, and I don't believe it now."

"You said murder," I repeated.

"If it wasn't an accident, and it sure as hell wasn't suicide, what else is there? Especially now! Asey turning up conveniently dead just after he's been shooting his mouth off to the press in an interview that's 'to be continued'?" When I looked at him dumbly, he went on with impatience. "Wake up, Cindy! Ever since Dan died, since the very night he vanished, Asey was telling everyone there'd been foul play. Nobody took him seriously. He'd been talking again now, since the fire here, since the poltergeist disturbance, and people *were* listening. The Gloucester newspaper ran a continuing feature. The TV stations came looking for him and couldn't find him. Do you think his turning up dead was a coincidence?"

I shook my head.

"I didn't think so," Paul said with a trace of his old sardonic manner. "The way you were poking into things, and putting your head together with Rhodes. You thought Dan's death was fishy too. So does Lissa. Poor kid," he said heavily, "nobody takes her seriously either."

"And Asey was a drunk who went around talking about ghost boats."

"That wasn't all." Paul looked at me directly. "I know what it was Asey'd been keeping secret. You know how Dan's supposed to have gone out because of an emergency phone call he received? There wasn't any."

I stared.

"Asey was here," Paul repeated. "It was a lousy night, and Asey just missed running into a tree up around the bend. He decided he'd better stop here and ask Dan and Elizabeth to put him up. When he saw the lights were all out, he let himself in. He knows this house inside and out." Then he stopped. "He *did* know. It's going to be hard getting used to the idea he's gone."

"Go on," I said gently.

"He was in here when the clock struck three, and he was cold sober. A sad condition he was trying to remedy by going through Dan's liquor supply. When you drink as much as Asey did, it takes a long time to hit the dull glow stage, and Asey hadn't hit it yet when he heard Dan come down the stairs. He didn't think Dan would appreciate stumbling over him, so he kept quiet in a corner. The point is, he was in the house for over an hour, and in his right mind, and the telephone never rang. So whyever Dan went out that night, it wasn't because he got a phone call."

"And then ... Asey went out in the harbor too?"

"After a while he got worried about Dan. And probably by that time the liquor was having an effect. Asey decided to go and look for him. He rowed out to the mooring pole," Paul said harshly, "switched over to Dan's little outboard, and went out into the storm. And when he found the *Sea Witch*, he couldn't get Dan to see him. The mist was thick, and the waves—What Asey remembered was darting around trying to signal to the *Sea Witch* with a lantern, and then this 'ghost boat' bearing down. He ran into the *Sea Witch* trying to get out of the ghost boat's way. Dan must have felt the crash. He sheered off toward shore, and the ghost boat took off after him. And Asey went into the nearest dock, found a car with its doors unlocked, and slept it off."

"Didn't you tell any of this to the authorities?"

"When I got here, which wasn't till the day after Dan was found, the authorities had already labeled the death accidental drowning and Elizabeth had had Dan cremated. Lissa was practically catatonic, Elizabeth was glued together by sheer willpower, and Asey was on a week-long bender. When he sobered up, he told me the story. He also told me that Dan had had a lot of ledgers and legal papers spread out on his desk that night, so whatever drove Dan out into the teeth of the storm, it must have been tied to something that he'd found."

I remembered what Elizabeth had said about how troubled Dan had been for some days before his death.

"You never told," I said. Paul shook his head.

"Who'd have believed me? I wasn't here. All I had was hearsay evidence from an old crock, and a well-known grudge against the whole Rockcove Hall situation. So I made Asey swear a Bible oath he wouldn't tell anyone else what he'd told me. He may have been a drinker, but he took his religion very seriously. And I swore to him that as soon as I found some evidence the police would take seriously, I'd make them reopen the case."

Illumination struck me. "*That's* why you were so insistent about not going back to college. About staying here and operating the *Sea Witch* as a charter."

"You got it. The *Sea Witch* makes a good cover." He looked at me, then away. "I do like working with boats. But I would probably have gone back to school this year if it weren't for Dan's death. Now I've been here a year, and what have I accomplished? I still don't know how Dan died, or why. I've fallen for a girl. There's a bunch of assorted spirits wreaking havoc on Rockcove Hall. And Asey's dead."

"Maybe that's not all." I took both of his hands in mine. "You have me working on it too. You can have Bill if you want him. A junior reporter, and an outsider—that's a good cover too. Can't reporters poke into things ordinary citizens can't? And if you're right about Asey's death, something has changed. Somebody's getting afraid, or running out of time."

"At least you said some*body*, not some*thing*," Paul said, and smiled at me. Then he rose. "We'd better drop this for now and get back to the others."

They were all at dinner except for Lissa. "She wouldn't come down," Ailsa said flatly.

I went up and found her hunched on her bed, staring out the window. She dragged her eyes with difficulty to focus on me, and her voice was an even monotone. "Asey's dead, isn't he? Nobody will tell me."

"Yes, he's dead. He was unconscious, and he drowned. He didn't suffer. He didn't know what was happening."

"I knew it would happen," Lissa said. She said it as if she were telling me the sun would rise tomorrow. I looked at her, shocked, and she drew a shuddering breath. "I think of things, and then they happen. Daddy getting killed in the storm and Asey dying. But I didn't make those things happen, did I, Cindy?"

"Of course not!" I wrapped her in my arms. Then I groped my way carefully. "What—kind of things *can* you make happen? Did you tie a string to Mike's chair and pull it? Or shortsheet the Gasses' bed? You can tell me."

"You don't understand." There was that phrase again. "I didn't *do* the things. I only wished something would happen . . . to get even with them for mocking the Watcher. Or to make Mom not marry Steve. And then those things— happened."

"The Watcher?" I asked innocently, while my heart was pounding.

But that was absolutely all that she would say. I

stayed with her until she fell asleep—with the light on, of course—and went downstairs to discover that in my absence the poltergeist had again been active.

Nineteen

There was nothing spectacular this time. Just the usual brownout, candles going out, and beach pebbles flung onto the tables. The police heard about it when they came back the next day to report the result of the autopsy on Asey Dawson. One of them asked pointedly whether we had any disturbed children on the premises.

The autopsy result was death by accidental drowning while intoxicated. And that was that. Case closed, except for the question of what to do with the remains. Asey had no known kin.

"We'll take care of it," Elizabeth said after a glance at Paul. "Funeral, and—everything." She made an inconclusive gesture. "Oh, I just don't see how... Paul, will you—?"

I went with Paul to see the undertaker. Asey was cremated, as Dan had been. His ashes would be buried in the Lancaster plot. We all went to the memorial service in the white wooden church, even Kevin and Lissa, and listened to the minister read the Mariners' Psalm: *They that go down to the sea in ships, that do business in great waters...*

Some of the later words struck me forcibly. . . . *Their soul is melted because of trouble. They reel to and fro, and stagger like a drunken man, and are at their wit's end.* I stole a glance at Paul and felt his fingers tighten around my hand.

Rockporters and tourists and a couple of reporters showed up at the service too. Mr. Martin was prominent, snapping pictures even in the cemetery. I shouldn't let it bother me, I thought over a stab of anger. Asey would probably have gotten a kick out of it.

As reporters closed in on Elizabeth and Paul afterward, Bill came over. "Can't an old friend get you out of here for a little while? My uncle's sending me over to the Hammond Museum. He gives it a plug once every summer, and he hoped I could come up with a fresh angle. Come on, it will do you good."

I searched for an excuse to avoid having to tell him what had happened between Paul and me. "Elizabeth—"

"Elizabeth," Bill said, "has McGovern looking after her proprietarily. Ailsa has the kids. Lancaster has the TV crew. Maybe he'll punch them out. That should make him feel better." Then his tone changed. "It's okay, Cindy. I saw you two together at the service. We're still friends, aren't we? You're not getting rid of me as easily as all that."

So I went with Bill back down the road toward Gloucester, and the break did help me. The Hammond Castle Museum was an incongruity, a pseudo-castle built by an early twentieth-century inventor. Into it Mr. Hammond had placed all his cherished artifacts from around the world, and there was no common denominator, no common scale.

"What an inventive mind," Bill said, grinning. "They always seem a little weird to ordinary people." He ran around making notes, and I sat in the courtyard underneath gracious trees and waited. Mr. Hammond might have been a great philanthropist and creator, the inventor of remote control devices, among other things, but it was nature, not his creations, that brought me peace.

It was a peace that lasted until we were back again at the hall, closeted with Paul in his room— the one place we felt safe from being overheard. "If Kevin hears anything, which he won't because he's outside swimming, it won't matter. That kid lets things roll off him." Paul looked at me. "Did you tell Rhodes?"

"Not yet. I thought you'd want to."

So Paul told Bill, too, about Asey and the night Dan disappeared. Bill frowned.

"I think you're right. There must have been something in those papers that made your brother go out in the boat. Something that wouldn't wait till morning. There were no electric wires down; I checked. And the road wasn't closed. Besides, Elizabeth heard him talking on the phone. So, if the phone didn't ring, then *he* must have placed the call. The person on the other end must have told him the road was closed so he'd take the *Sea Witch* out. Can you get your hands on those papers Asey saw?"

"I'll find a way," Paul said shortly.

"I'm going to do some research on poltergeists and magic tricks," I said. Paul shot me a glowering look, and I added quickly, "Lissa said she didn't *do* anything, and I believe her. She believes she wished the things into happening. But I know she didn't."

"Did you pick that up by vibrations?" Paul asked sarcastically.

"Don't joke about it." I turned to Bill. "You were going to get into old material on Dan and the hall in the newspaper morgue. Is there a way of getting police and autopsy reports?"

"Like Lancaster said, 'I'll find a way.' "

Paul's eyes fixed us. "We don't tell anyone anything. Understood? Not even Elizabeth, till we have some solid proof. She's in no shape to handle our suspicions."

So that was that, until we turned up—what had Paul called it?—solid proof. And meanwhile life went on. New guests kept arriving, needing to be taken care of. Fortunately—or unfortunately, depending on your point of view—they were hardy souls attracted by the drama of Rockcove Hall. Asey's death was like an added fillip. We had another incident of candles mysteriously flickering out at dinner, but nothing—I caught my breath when I found myself thinking the words—nothing grisly happened.

Ailsa was preparing for a special gallery exhibition down in Boston. Steve was trying to persuade Elizabeth to marry him and leave Rockport, and Elizabeth still acted as if she didn't hear. She was like a sleepwalker most of the time. So, to my dismay, was Lissa. Kevin was much as always, but both children behaved as if Asey's death had never happened.

Whether they were by now inured to shock, or whether defense mechanisms shielded them from full realization, I did not know. "I wish I had their resilience," Elizabeth said once, looking after them. "And yet, I wonder."

That was one of the few times she seemed to be tuned in to what was going on. I could hear her walking the floor at night, and then she'd be drugged with sleep, or perhaps tranquilizers, by day. That frightened me, but I didn't want to upset her precarious balance. I did talk to Ailsa, and Ailsa was reassuring. "She has an excellent doctor. He knows what he's doing. Elizabeth's in shock; all this has brought back everything she didn't make peace with after Dan's accident."

I didn't challenge the word *accident*, and I didn't see Ailsa much because of the work she was doing for her show. With her not around, and with Elizabeth ill, it was Paul and I who were running Rockcove Hall.

It seemed so strange, and strangely, it seemed so right. And that showed how far we'd both come since we'd first met. Our personality conflicts, our differences in viewpoint, dwindled in importance in contrast to the immensity of the tasks we'd set ourselves. We had Martha and Ella doing cooking and housekeeping; we could always turn to Steve McGovern; we could call on Bill. But it was Paul and I who had to make the real decisions; it was Paul and I who had the real ties to Rockcove Hall. It was romantic, but it was far more than that as well. We were in sync. We had a rhythm.

July went away inexorably into August. Ailsa's new works went on display at the Craig Gallery, a preview of her autumn show in New York. She herself left for a few weeks in Taos, New Mexico. The responsibilities of Rockcove Hall settled even

more heavily on Paul and me. I was worried about
Lissa, who was growing steadily more withdrawn;
I was worried about Elizabeth too.

When Steve stopped by unexpectedly one night,
Elizabeth could not even make the effort to come
down to see him. Paul wasn't there, but I took
Steve up to my sitting room for a serious talk. I
told him how concerned I was about Elizabeth's
condition, and he frowned.

"I know. I'm worried too. I've tried to talk sense
into her, but she won't listen. She won't give me a
straight answer about our getting married either,"
he added grimly. "As soon as Labor Day's over, I
intend to make her come away with me for a rest.
A cruise, maybe. Ailsa will keep the children.
Exactly what has the doctor said about Elizabeth?"

"That's just it. I don't know. Elizabeth won't talk
about it, and she's gone back to him only once. He
increased the frequency of the tranquilizers and
gave her sleeping pills. I know that because I
looked at the labels on the bottles," I admitted.
"But I have no idea whether she's taking them
when she's supposed to. Elizabeth hates popping
pills."

"Elizabeth," said Steve, "hates anyone telling
her what to do."

Our eyes met in rueful understanding, but a
chill shook me. Elizabeth had never needed to be
told what to do before. She had been everyone
else's peace and wisdom. Now the world was
turned inside out.

Mr. Ikawa left after pressing his business card
upon me. Other guests came and went. Paul went
on the search for Dan's papers, and came up

empty. He couldn't ask Elizabeth for them without giving an explanation.

"Have you tried the attic?" I asked. "She could have put them there, since it's always locked." We got the key, but when we reached the door, we found it unlocked. I told Paul about my previous experience. He changed the lock, frowning heavily. We did find some legal files in the attic, and they were untouched; dust lay heavily upon them.

I spent my day off in the Gloucester library, reading up on poltergeists and related phenomena. It started to rain while I was there. When I arrived back late for dinner a sodden mess, Paul greeted me with an odd expression. "I've found Dan's case notes. And Rhodes called. He wants to come over after dinner."

We convened, as before, in Paul's room. He lit a fire. "We've forgotten something important," Bill said without preamble. He emptied a manila envelope on the table. "I brought them before, the day Cindy found Dawson's body. They've been under the seat of my car ever since."

They were Mr. Ikawa's photographs. I looked, and felt something turn over in me.

"So there *was* somebody out on the rocks that night," Paul muttered, studying a print. Mr. Ikawa's new no-flash-needed film lived up to his expectations. A womanly shape, copper-clad, was clearly visible.

"That means she wasn't supernatural," I whispered. "Ghosts would be ectoplasm; they wouldn't photograph except with—what's that special photography parapsychologists use?"

"Kirlian photography. It's based on electric impulses," Paul said. "Look at the other picture. The close-up one."

There *had* been an unmanned powerboat in operation in the harbor. If not on the night Dan died, at least on the night Mr. Ikawa took his picture.

"When was this?" I asked suddenly. "Was it around the date the coroner said Asey died?"

We stared at one another as the implications washed over us.

"That's something else," Bill said soberly. "I managed to get into the police files, and I made an illegal copy." He brought it out. "There were bruises on the back of Asey's head and neck, and on his shoulders. The conclusion was that they were made by rocks when the body rolled around. Before death took place. The point is, Dan's body had them too."

"Nobody caught that?" I exclaimed.

"If anybody did, they chalked it up to coincidence," Paul said with sarcasm. "We're getting near something. But we still can't prove murder. Simpson would laugh us out of the police station." He leaned over the photographs intently. "How the hell did somebody do this? If we knew how, maybe we'd know who."

"You found something today, didn't you?" I asked him.

Paul shrugged. "I found an *absence* of something. There's nothing in those legal files that could remotely justify Dan's tearing across the harbor in a storm. Either the matter was too sensitive for him to record on paper, or it had nothing to do with his law practice." He shook his head. "How about you, Lucinda?" He'd taken to calling me by my full name in affectionate teasing.

I produced some candles and lighted them. "Now watch."

In ten minutes they went out as the candles on our dinner table had, snuffed by an invisible hand. Bill whistled. "How?"

"Easy. You just run a skewer or something in from one side, through the wick, so the cord is severed. It won't show if you seal the hole with a lighted match. When the candle burns down to that point, it just goes out. You can pull a chair over by running fishing line around its leg ahead of time at floor level, and then pulling. You can knock tables and vases over with a yardstick fastened to your shoe with elastic. In a dim room who'd notice? You can send pebbles through the air with a slingshot. What I don't know is how the Watcher materializes on the rocks. No one from the hall could get there without being seen."

"No one from here?" Paul challenged.

"Who else has a reason?"

"The development company? They've been calling again, haven't they?" Paul asked acutely.

"Do they need the place badly enough to resort to that? Yes, they've been calling." I didn't add that the mystery caller had been phoning too.

"I've been checking on the developer, CJG," Bill reported. "They're in good financial shape. But they've been buying up other parcels around here, and some other firms have too. I couldn't find who owns those other firms." He paused significantly. "CJG has openly admitted that they'd like to put up a shopping center here."

We looked at one another. "In other words"

—Paul voiced what I was thinking—"some people
could have been speculating, maybe going over
their heads with mortgages, knowing they could
turn over big profits from the developers once
Rockcove Hall was sold. Because eliminating
Rockcove Hall would be crucial to the shopping
center going up."

In other words, the list of potential suspects was
a mile long again. And all anonymous.

"We've got to get the names of those company
owners," I started to say. And was interrupted by a
crash. It wasn't happening down in the public
rooms. It was happening across the hall.

Twenty

We raced to where the sound had come from—
Lissa's room. Her door was locked and no one
answered at out shouting. I unlocked my door,
hurried through the sitting room, the bedroom,
the connecting bathroom. Lissa's room, for the
first time, was all in darkness. The lamp and its
small table had crashed to the floor. Beyond the
broken glass Lissa stood rigid, staring out.

"Lissa! *Lissa! Look* at me!" I shook her, slapped
her gently.

"Never mind that," Paul said grimly, looking
past us through the window. "Put her to bed in
your room. And lock yourselves in! Our lady friend's
doing her routine on the rocks again."

He and Bill rushed out. I drew the window
shade as if I could shut out ghosts, and carried
Lissa into my room and laid her on the bed. I
wrapped her in blankets and then, when nothing
seemed to reach her, lay down beside her and
wrapped her in my arms. She revived at last, but
only to a kind of stupor.

Paul and Bill returned, carrying a tray with cups

and a steaming teapot. "Gone," Paul said briefly. "And where the devil it vanished to, Lord only knows. We lost it by the dock." He lifted Lissa and forced her to look straight at him. "Did you hear me, Lissa? There *was* something out there, but it was something human! Not the Watcher."

Lissa just gazed back, mutely obstinate.

"I'm not getting through to her," I wailed childishly after Bill was gone. "I thought I could once, but now—Elizabeth relied on me, and I'm no good at all. . . ."

"Cindy, stop it! You relied on Elizabeth, and you can't anymore. Are you holding that against her? Maybe we ought to send the kids away from Rockport. There must be some other relatives they could visit. We've got to get her rational enough tomorrow to discuss it."

But we didn't. Because when I took a breakfast tray to Elizabeth's room, I first could not get in, and then I could not rouse her. Even the drastic measures I'd used before did not work. I shouted for Paul, heedless of the paying guests, and Paul phoned the doctor.

There was no Ailsa to come help this time. Nor Steve, who was away for two weeks on a business trip. We were on our own. It was on my own I had to answer Lissa when she waited for me in my room after the doctor left.

"She's going to die, isn't she?" she said flatly.

"*Elizabeth?* Oh, honey, no!" Resolutely I willed my face not to betray what the doctor had told me, that Elizabeth had come dangerously close to overdosing on her sleeping pills. I knelt down by Lissa, walking on eggs so as not to transgress her careful adult dignity. "Lissa, she had an accident.

It can happen sometimes when someone's taking strong prescription drugs. But she's not going to die."

"Not till next time. It will happen," Lissa said as if she'd read the future. "What will happen then to me and Kevin?"

"Lissa, don't talk like that! I swear to you, I won't *let* there be a next time."

How I would achieve that, I did not know. It was Paul who supplied the answer. Paul cornered me in the kitchen after lunch and said bluntly, "We've got to get her away from here now."

"How?"

"First we've got to get her another doctor. She must have been seeing someone back in Waltham before they moved here. We've got to get him to order her to a hospital off the cape. She should be safe there. You're a blood relation, so you'd better be the one to call the doctor."

"How are we going to find him?"

Paul shrugged. "There must be records somewhere."

There weren't any in the attic. In Elizabeth's own room I finally found a file cabinet in a closet. The locked drawer, which I opened with Elizabeth's keys, contained a strongbox that I coolly carried away to inspect later. There were papers relating to the sale of the Waltham house and the move to Rockcove Hall. I took those, too, while Elizabeth slumbered. Finally I found boxes of canceled checks.

I searched rapidly for the ones from the last year Dan and Elizabeth had lived in Waltham. Checks in Elizabeth's and Dan's handwriting to department stores, supermarkets, the IRS, insurance companies, the gas and electric and telephone

companies. Finally a few checks to a Dr. J.W.
Campbell.

We had a Boston area telephone book at the
registration desk. Dr. J.W. Campbell was an intern-
ist in family practice. Paul guarded my privacy
while I phoned.

'Yes, of course I remember Elizabeth Lancaster.
I'm sorry to hear she's ill. You're her cousin, you
say? I don't know—"

"Doctor, please. We must have a second opin-
ion, and Elizabeth's too sick to call you herself.
She almost died last night from a drug reaction."

The doctor's voice changed. "Mrs. Lancaster
has always been very cautious about taking medication. I can be up there around four P.M. tomorrow."

Elizabeth was awake, though groggy. I told her
what I had done. She seemed relieved.

Then it was a case of waiting. I invaded Elizabeth's
strongbox and read her will to find out for myself
who would become the children's guardian if anything happened to their mother: it would be Ailsa
Craig. After I'd put the strongbox away, Steve
phoned. Paul answered and told him only that
Elizabeth was asleep. I looked at him. "You don't
suspect Steve?"

"Right now I don't trust anybody," Paul replied.

The Watcher walked on the point again that
night. I thanked God that Lissa did not know it.
She was in my bed, and the shades were drawn.
Again Paul and Bill went out looking and came
back frustrated.

I awoke in the middle of the night to find Lissa
sitting up but silent, and Deborah in bed with us,
her tail gently wagging. "I want to know what's
happening," Lissa said uncompromisingly.

"There's another doctor coming to see your mother tomorrow. Dr. Campbell, from Waltham. Do you remember him?" She nodded. "Lissa, I truly believe things are going to get better now."

All at once the beneficent presence was in the room with us again. I saw the shifting pattern in the mirror. The presence was trying to comfort us, to bring us warning. I found myself possessed by an overwhelming sadness that was only partly my own. And at the foot of the bed Deborah's tail wagged and wagged.

In the morning everything was brighter. I made Lissa promise not to tell anyone about the doctor coming. She nodded gravely. Downstairs a group of guests was besieging Paul to take them out in the *Sea Witch*, a task he'd been avoiding lately. No matter how much he detested playing nursemaid to the tourists, a day on the water would do him good. "Go ahead. Take a picnic basket, and keep them out for lunch. I can manage here without you."

"I'll get you for that, Lucinda." Paul made a swat at me, but his face looked more cheerful. Mr. Martin, passing by and seeing the clinch that followed, smirked.

Mr. Martin was a problem. The poltergeist's visits had inspired him to remain with us all summer. Now he was getting bored. The poltergeist activity had become old hat, and not all new arrivals appreciated him playing expert. What was worse, he was developing the habit of dogging Paul's heels and mine.

When he followed me to the registration desk after lunch and inquired whether there had been any further TV interest in Rockcove Hall, my patience snapped.

"If you're finding life too dull here, please let me know. We could use some extra rooms next weekend."

"Oh, no, no. I fully expect to finish the summer here." He tittered. "That is, if the hall's staying open. With Mrs. Lancaster not quite on top of things, so to speak, the responsibilities must be a burden for a young girl like you. Especially under the circumstances..." He looked pointedly at a photograph of Paul that I'd taken and propped up on the desk, and swept me a little bow. "Good day, Miss Clayborne. Or should I say, the captain's lady?"

A wave of color swept over me. "Is that supposed to mean something?" I asked frigidly.

"Oh, nothing. Nothing at all, my dear young lady. Merely a pleasantry." His eyes were bright and malicious behind his glasses. "By the way, I'm having some of my latest paintings shipped here. You will keep an eye out for them, won't you? I want to take them round to the Castell Gallery. But you must know the place well, don't you?"

"No."

"You should pay it a visit sometime soon. It should have a special appeal to you."

The memory of my arrival flooded over me. Of how I had turned into the gallery with my heavy suitcase. And the woman's reaction, the reaction I'd gotten everywhere when I'd said I was on my way to Rockcove Hall.

I ran out to the car and drove straight to the Castell Gallery.

It was dim inside, polished and orderly. The air,

as I entered, became charged, the way rooms did sometimes at Rockcove Hall. . . . I went, unseeing, past the carved driftwood sea gulls, the watercolors, and the decoys, past oil paintings new and old. Straight to the far corner of the second room, with all my senses tingling.

The American primitive, painted on wood as were many early works, showed a young woman scarcely older than myself, a woman with sad eyes and rippling hair, whose copper glints echoed the matching color of her silk gown.

"Quite a resemblance, isn't it?" Mrs. Castell said behind me. "I noticed it the first day you came in."

"Who is she?" I asked through dry lips.

"I thought you knew. That's Lucinda Clayborne Lancaster."

Twenty-one

But I'm Lucinda Clayborne! The words leaped to
my brain, but fortunately not to my lips. What I
did say, very civilized and controlled, was, "No,
really? One of the Lancasters of Rockcove Hall?"

"She's the 'captain's lady' the tourists are so het
up about. We've had day trippers off the bus in
here asking the way to the hall so they could go
and gawk. Bunch of ghouls, all of them," she
added, "but the way I feel is, we're going to be
stuck with tourists anyway, so we might as well
make good money off them. If they want to believe in poltergeists, that's their privilege. It can't
hurt us."

"You don't think the hall has a poltergeist, then?"
I ventured.

"If I shouted ghost every time this place creaked
and something got knocked over, I'd never have
made it through my childhood. All these old houses
have creaks and drafts. Ben Simpson says what
you had at the hall had something to do with the
tides, and he should know. He was with the Coast
Guard before he joined the police. It's too bad

about what happened to poor old Asey," Mrs.
Castell added, "but it's no surprise. Just hard luck
for the Lancasters it had to happen at the hall. I'm
glad it seems to be helping business there. Asey'd
probably enjoy that. He was no end riled up when
we started hearing stories about how Elizabeth
might have to sell out. It would be a shame to see
that beautiful old place go out of the family, let
alone be torn down."

"Is the captain's lady's name—and what she
looked like—common knowledge?" I asked faintly.
Mrs. Castell snorted.

"You don't see reporters beating my door down
to photograph that painting, do you? I doubt most
people know the picture exists. I like to know the
provenance of antiques I sell. That picture was
originally part of a pair. When they came in, I
checked the tombstones in the cemetery. She was
Lucinda Clayborne Lancaster, and she lived here
for only a year, back in—what was it?—1803 or
1804. Her husband's name was Daniel Seth
Lancaster, and he brought her here from some-
place down south."

"Daniel?" My mouth was dry.

"Lots of the old families like to perpetuate the
same first names. I had the pair of paintings; they
came in with a bunch of stuff from the hall a few
years ago. The portrait of the captain sold right
away, but there's some damage on this one that's
lowered its value for collectors." She showed me
an area in one corner where the wood had been
waterstained and some amateur artist had attempted
an unsuccessful touch-up.

I gazed at the picture, and a trick of the mind
superimposed other images upon it. Myself, the

first night of the poltergeist, wearing the copper
gown I had been led to. The figure beyond the
windows. The figure in the snapshots. The figure
in my mirror . . .

I wrenched my eyes away, gazing blankly at a
wall of shelves so the gallery owner would not see
me cry.

She thought she knew what I was looking at.
"Those old floats are nice, aren't they? Come to
think of it, they're part of the Rockcove Hall lot
too."

My vision focused , blurred, then cleared. They
weren't the same. They were simply very similar
spherical glass balls, faintly iridescent, one of them
seawater color, one lavender.

"What are they?" I whispered.

"Floats. Fishermen used to use them on their
smaller nets. Collectors' items now, of course.
Those are quite nice ones. The Craig Gallery has
some too. I can make you a good price if you're
interested."

No, I didn't want them. But the portrait—

"How much is the painting?" I heard my own
voice asking.

My family had given me some spending-and-
emergency money for the summer, and I also had
the salary Elizabeth was paying me. I wrote out a
check, and Mrs. Castell wrapped the wood panel
in tissue and handed it to me.

"Tell Elizabeth I'm glad the hall's doing well.
She's a nice woman, and a good artist. I wouldn't
mind having some of her work to sell, but the
Craig Gallery always handles it."

"Is there something wrong about that?" I asked,
startled by the amusement on her face.

"Oh, no. It's a fine gallery," Mrs. Castell said hastily. "It's just that—oh, well, I'll say it; it's common knowledge after all. Ailsa Craig was going to marry Dan Lancaster before he met Elizabeth. And a year or so ago it looked like things were finally going to work out for her with Steve McGovern. But then Dan died..." She let the sentence hang significantly. "And Elizabeth and Ailsa are best of friends. Funny world, isn't it?"

I just nodded and got myself out to the car. My mind was whirling, and it was several minutes before I trusted myself to drive.

Lucinda Clayborne Lancaster. Nearly two hundred years ago there had been another girl in my father's family with the same first name as mine, who had loved and wed a Daniel Lancaster. My father had wed my mother, who had a cousin who also married a Daniel Lancaster. Both Dan Lancasters were seafaring men, so the fact that they both died on the rocks was probability, not fate.

The figure I had seen in the mirror, the figure someone was trying to make us believe was walking on the rocks, was, like me, a Lucinda Clayborne. Scientists were investigating the theory that strong emotions were a kind of electric energy that could live on in the molecules of the wood and stone at the place where they had been felt. Something genetic in me must have picked up the emotional memory of Rockcove Hall.

That did not explain the poltergeist. That did not explain the figure beyond the window. They were in no way related to the Watcher, whose sad, reassuring presence I knew now I had felt.

There were other things I'd learned during the

visit to the gallery, but I pushed them away to deal with later.

I went back to the hall and straight to Elizabeth's room. She was resting; the doctor was just about due. "Why didn't you tell me the captain's lady was named Lucinda Clayborne?"

Elizabeth pushed herself up on the pillows, looking startled. "I never knew! Dan always just called her the captain's lady. How did you find out?"

In answer I unwrapped the painting. Elizabeth's eyes changed. "Dear God," she breathed.

"You've never seen this before, have you?" I took a deep breath and said gently, "It came from here. Mrs. Castell bought it, probably when Dan's grandfather's estate was being settled."

"Dan never told me," Elizabeth said wonderingly. "I know I never saw that picture in this house. I'd remember . . . But there's so much I don't seem to be remembering, isn't there?"

"There was another, matching painting, Elizabeth. Her husband. Daniel Seth Lancaster."

"Dan was named for his grandfather, who was named for an ancestor. It must have been the"— she swallowed hard—"the captain."

I didn't have to comment. There was a knock on the door, and Lissa came in. "Dr. Campbell's here to see Mom," she said. Then she froze, staring at the painting.

Elizabeth's hand reached for her. "That's one of your ancestors. And one of Cindy's too. We're related twice over. Isn't that—special?"

Lissa's eyes jerked to me, and I trembled at what I saw there. Abruptly she burst into tears and ran out. I rose to follow, but Elizabeth's fingers caught me. "No. Let her come to you. She will, now...."

Her voice trailed off. The doctor entered, a heavyset man with a quiet authority. "I'll want to give Mrs. Lancaster a thorough examination. And I want to see her medication."

"It's on the table. And my cousin stays," Elizabeth said. The exertion she'd been making had tired her, but she seemed less apprehensive in the doctor's presence. He sat on the bed to check her blood pressure, heartbeat, and pulse. Then he looked closely at her eyes and snapped to me.

"Where's her medication?"

I brought the pills silently. He read the labels, then shook a few pills from each container into his hand. Then his whole manner alerted.

"This Valium's twice as strong as the label specifies. And the other pills are pure caffeine! No wonder she's been feeling like she was jumping out of her skin, or worse. These aren't the pills her doctor prescribed. Who could have tampered with them?"

I stared at him, appalled. "We've all of us been in here. Me; Dan's brother, Paul; the children. The cook or waitress come up sometimes too."

"Not anymore," he said firmly, and reached for the telephone. "I'm sending her to a Boston hospital. They'll send an ambulance to pick her up."

He wasn't even trusting a local ambulance.... "Could I speak to you a moment, Doctor?" I asked hoarsely. And then, when we were isolated in the corner, I said, "Tell me one thing. Could what she's been taking have killed her?"

"If it continued, possibly." He eyed me keenly.

"You've had some unexplained deaths around here, haven't you?"

I realized with a shock that for the first time, a responsible authority figure was agreeing with Paul's and my suspicions.

Twenty-two

I stayed with Elizabeth, and I packed her bag. When the ambulance came an hour later, I went downstairs with the stretcher bearers. I kissed her and promised to look after the children and Rockcove Hall. By now the sedative the doctor had given her was already taking effect. She nodded drowsily.

The ambulance left. I went back into a quiet house. Paul had taken my suggestion literally and was treating the guests to an all-day excursion. Everyone had gone, including Kevin and Mr. Martin. Only the kitchen staff was here. And Lissa, at a table on the dining porch doing watercolors. I went to my rooms and spread the pieces of evidence we'd accumulated so far out on my table. The photographs. The copies of the autopsy reports. The police reports on the two fatal accidents. Dan's client papers—I leafed through them, feeling unethical, and came to the same conclusion as had Paul. They didn't hold the clue to why Dan had left the hall on the night he died.

Next I transferred my attention to the contents of Elizabeth's filing cabinet. Copies of the deed to

Rockcove Hall—the original was probably in a bank somewhere. Copies of wills—Dan's grandfather's, Dan's, Elizabeth's. Under the first, made before Dan had married, Paul would have inherited the hall if Dan died without heirs. Dan's and Elizabeth's wills left their property totally to each other, or, in the event of both spouses' death, to their children. Ailsa was appointed the children's guardian. In the event of Kevin's or Lissa's death without heirs, the share of the deceased child would go to Paul. Both Dan's will and Elizabeth's named Steve McGovern as executor. Of course, I'd been told he was Dan's investment counselor.

There he was, in a photograph of Dan's graduating class from Harvard Law School. No wonder he felt competent to give Elizabeth advice, I thought absently, and went on looking. A paper giving Steve power of attorney so he could handle Dan's investments without Dan's own signature. Records of stock and bond sales. It was all a foreign language to me. I turned again to the police reports of the two deaths, and then to the books I'd brought from Gloucester.

They were not only on poltergeists, I'd discovered. They dealt with other occult phenomena as well, and as I read, I grew increasingly uneasy.

Ever since the night of the first poltergeist activity, I'd been bothered by the idea that there were so many "ghostly" phenomenon occurring at the same time. Now I had more to add to the list: a ghost boat. An entity who walked upon the rocks and yet appeared when I needed her, bringing comfort, leading, warning. And something, or somebody, who unlocked locked doors and created drafts.

There was nothing in any of the books about so

many different phenomena happening in one place and time. There was a great deal about how one dominant phenomenon usually accelerated to a shocking climax if not stopped—usually a fire.

There was a draft on my neck, like fingers trailing, and the sense of presence was strong and urgent. I listened to my instinct, not to reason. I set Lucinda Clayborne Lancaster's portrait on a chair and gazed at it until my vision blurred. Until the whole surface of the painting was one copper shimmer. *All right, Lucinda . . . you're trying to tell me something. Show me now. Before it's too late.*

I don't know where those words came from, they simply leaped into my mind. I closed my eyes for a moment, and when I opened them, the expression on the portrait's features seemed to have changed. I rose and went downstairs, and it was as if it had been that other time, when I found Asey's body. Someone—Lucinda Lancaster—was moving in me, bidding my feet to carry me to the shore. To the place where I had found the body. And then inland, along the crevasse in the rocks. Until I saw what I had not seen before. What no one had seen, because no one had looked.

There was a kind of crevice in the rock wall, a crevice that grew larger when the rock before it moved, at my bidding, easily away. A cave . . . no, a passageway. All the tales I'd ever read about old smugglers' lairs leaped to my mind. But my body moved steadily, carefully, inexorably into the passage. Followed it around a turn and around again, and upward.

I was in total darkness now. I moved by touch. My fingers explored the rocks before me, and moved upward. To a wooden ceiling, and a trap-door.

I pushed it open and, finding toeholds, pulled myself up too.

I was in the carriage house, in a windowless room behind the front area's back wooden wall. Some light came dimly through cracks around that connecting, unhandled door, and through the roof. It was enough to show the pile of copper silk folded on the floor.

I knew even before I found the telltale berry stain on the bodice that it was the gown I had worn the night of the disastrous dinner.

Someone had been using the gown to create the apparition of the Watcher. But how was the "ghost" getting in and out of the carriage house? Not from the sea. He or she might be seen. Using the carriage house door, which could be viewed from Granite Street and the hall, would be too risky. I sat and thought, holding the copper dress to me like a talisman, but my thoughts led nowhere. And at last, reluctantly, I crept with the dress back through the passageway. Replacing the stone at the entrance carefully, I thrust the dress beneath my shirt and literally crawled along the ground till I was past the dock and up again on the lawn.

Just in time. When I stood, feeling self-conscious, to brush myself off, I found the *Sea Witch* at her mooring and Paul ferrying the first batch of pas-sengers in by motorboat.

He saw me and waved, and I waved back and stood waiting. The guests, including Mr. Martin, came past me curiously, but did not stop. Paul went back to the *Sea Witch* twice more. Then at last we were alone on the lower lawn, and he came toward me. He did not reach out; he did not take me in his arms; we just stood looking at each other and I felt I had come home.

"Something's happened, hasn't it?"

"Yes. I can't tell you here. But, Paul—Elizabeth's now in a hospital in Boston."

It was not until after dinner that we could really talk. Paul had interested a number of the guests in driving to Gloucester for a movie. Somehow we managed to get everyone to go. Paul looked at me wryly. "Can we finally have a night for the two of us, or do we have to invite Rhodes?"

"We don't. But we may not have a very pleasant evening anyway. I have a lot to tell you. For starters, somebody'd switched Elizabeth's pills."

It started there, and it got worse. Paul looked at the portrait of Lucinda Clayborne Lancaster and frowned. "I don't know who sold this, but I'd bet it wasn't Dan. He had a thing about hanging on to family pieces. I'd never seen this one, by the way."

"Could it have been Steve McGovern? He was executor, and he had power of attorney."

"Not to sell family stuff. Dan would have killed him. Why were you standing on the lawn looking as though you'd seen a ghost when I came home?"

"You've got it backward," I said shakily. "I think a ghost led me to the proof our apparition was no ghost." I brought out the dress and described the passage to the carriage house. Paul looked sober.

"I've never seen it, but I'm not surprised. There are family stories about how this place was a station on the Underground Railroad. That room may have been used for hiding escaped slaves. The point is, whoever's been doing this has to know Rockcove Hall even better than the family. Dan

probably knew all about it, but not Elizabeth. If
she did, she wouldn't have been acting so"—he
fished for a phrase—"so haunted. Grandfather probably thought I was too young to tell. But who
would he have told?"

"Or who might have access to architectural draw-
ings of the hall? The developers?"

"Maybe. But I still can't see those guys setting
up an apparition. They're not that subtle."

"There was nothing terribly subtle about Elizabeth's medicine." I let out my breath. "I know . . .
we've been criminally negligent. Anybody's been
able to wander in and out of here. It's a public
business now. We locked the attic and the carriage
house, but not the medicine."

"And locks don't seem to have done any good
anyway." Paul straightened. "Let's see those papers you were telling me about."

We went up to my rooms.

I had read them all already, so I sat in the rocker
by the fire and scratched Deborah's ear. Deborah's
tail thumped, and a sense of presence grew. I had
no idea whether Paul could feel it. He was en-
grossed, and growing more uneasy by the minute.

When he was finished reading, it was very late.
He pushed his chair back and looked at me, and I
knew before he spoke what he was about to say.

"There's only one thing that makes sense in all
this. There *is* one person who was in a position to
do something that would make Dan troubled
enough, angry enough, to go out in that storm.
Somebody Dan would have phoned first to warn.
Somebody close enough for Dan not to have con-
fided even in Elizabeth, or to have left notes.
Steve McGovern."

"I can't believe it." But my voice was half-hearted.

"The investments, don't you remember? What a surprise it was to everyone that they were worth so little, and that Dan would have taken such a gamble? Steve had Dan's power of attorney. I was prelaw in college"—that was a little item I hadn't known—"and I've done just enough reading that that thing strikes me as fishy. I'm sure Dan meant to give Steve authorization within set limits. Maybe that paper's even a forgery. Maybe this whole courtship of Elizabeth is a cover-up so he won't be found out!"

I was appalled. "He *loves* Elizabeth."

"Maybe he does. Are you going to stand by and let her marry a murderer?"

"She hasn't said she would...and we don't know for sure he is."

"No, we need proof." Paul considered. "Steve's still away. We'd better get into *his* papers and have a look. Come on."

"Are you crazy? We can't leave Lissa and Kevin here alone. And we can't just break in."

"We'll take the kids to Martha Gibbs. She always stays up for the eleven o'clock news. If the police catch us, we can say Steve lent the place to us for privacy on dates."

I followed Paul docilely as he woke Lissa and swung Kevin over his shoulder, still half-asleep. Lissa just obeyed dumbly. We drove to Mrs. Gibbs, and explained we needed a sitter so we could do an important errand. She took one look at us and asked no questions.

And then we went to Steve McGovern's condo, and we picked the lock.

I couldn't believe we were doing this. I couldn't believe he was an embezzler or a murderer.

I couldn't believe it when the lights in the living room, where we were searching by flashlight, suddenly went on.

Steve McGovern was standing in the doorway, staring at us in disbelief. "If I may ask, what the hell do you think you're doing?"

"Looking for evidence of what you did to Dan," Paul said bluntly as I gasped. Before my eyes I saw Steve McGovern's face change into something that resembled Lissa's when she reached a moment against which she had been braced.

"I was afraid it would come out eventually," he said quietly.

I couldn't stop myself. "Are you admitting to *murder?*"

Steve stared at me. "What are you talking about? I invested Dan's money along with my own in some harebrained projects. *Now* I know they were harebrained. Then they seemed sure things. I lost his money, and I didn't have the guts to tell him what I'd done because he'd laid down definite parameters for his investments. So I started juggling paper to cover up. I thought I'd be able to recoup and replace the money before he found out." He took a deep breath. "Dan died before I was able to make it up. I still haven't been able to."

"Dan found out, didn't he?" Paul demanded. Steve nodded.

"He found out that night. He must have suspected earlier. He phoned and said he had to see me. He didn't say why, but somehow I knew." Steve indicated the wall of windows looking on the harbor.

"He was coming by boat because he'd found out somehow the road was closed. I told him it was too dangerous. I said whatever it was could wait till morning. But Dan, he always had a temper. It didn't wake easily, but when it did... I spent the whole night sitting here at the window watching for him, but he never came. And in the morning Elizabeth phoned, frantic, to say Dan had not come home."

"But you already knew that, didn't you?" Paul said in that same knifelike tone. Steve frowned at him.

"Is there something going on here I don't know about? I expected Dan to come and give me hell. He didn't. I expected to make financial restitution. I still do. I'm in love with Elizabeth, in case you don't know it. My wanting to marry her has nothing to do with this. And I fully intend to tell Elizabeth about all this before we marry. What I did was—unethical, but only on the margin of being actionable. I did have Dan's power of attorney. So if you're contemplating prosecution, Paul, I doubt you could. You don't have the necessary evidence."

Paul looked at him as if he couldn't believe what he was hearing. His face darkened. It was I who spoke.

"We're not contemplating embezzlement charges. We're contemplating a murder charge. And we do have evidence of that."

Twenty-three

"As God is my witness, I did not kill Dan. I cheated him out of his savings, yes. But not deliberately. And I certainly did not murder him, or Asey either."

We were sitting around Steve's kitchen table drinking coffee an hour later. We had told him about the autopsy reports, and how someone could have held the victims' heads beneath the water till they drowned, possibly after having drugged them first. That involved an explanation of Elizabeth's situation, and Steve was horror-struck.

"Someone tried to kill *her!*" He jumped up. "What hospital? I'm going to her."

"No, you're not," Paul said icily. "Not yet."

Steve offered to go to the police at once to tell all, taking us. Paul vetoed that too. I knew why. The "proof" I'd mentioned was still nebulous.

"What you need is to know what caused the *Sea Witch* to crack up that night." Steve was reading Paul's mind.

"What we need is to know who piloted Asey's ghost boat, and how," Paul corrected him. "We have proof now of its existence." He fixed Steve with a gimlet eye. "We'll go now. And in case you're thinking of pulling any fast ones, we've sent copies of all our evidence to Cindy's family's attorney. So our meeting with an unfortunate accident would change nothing."

"It's Elizabeth's safety that concerns me," Steve retorted.

We hadn't mailed any such copies, but we did so the first thing in the morning. It was a still, surreal day; the air was heavy, and the sky a dirty yellow. After a trip to the post office, which had a copying machine, we went back to the hall. Several guests were checking out by noon, and reservations were falling off, possibly because the Coast Guard weather station was predicting a storm.

I telephoned the hospital and was told Elizabeth was resting comfortably. I talked to Dr. Campbell and suggested she should be allowed no visitors. "I've already taken care of that," he said bluntly.

"Tell her"—I searched for words—"tell her I have proof somebody's been dressing up in Lucinda's silk dress to scare people. And I've found out how the poltergeist tricks are done." That would at least relieve Elizabeth of fears about her sanity. I did not, could not, say anything about Steve. Not yet.

Paul and I talked. "Steve didn't kill them," I said flatly, and Paul looked at me oddly.

"I agree with you. I don't know why. Gut-level instinct, I suppose. Can't you go off in one of your trances and get Lucinda the First to give us proof?"

"That isn't funny."

"I know it isn't," Paul said, and bent over to kiss me. By now I had told him about how Lucinda's presence had been guiding me, and he had not laughed. "The problem is, who else had a motive? Steve had plenty. The money business, and loving Elizabeth."

"Paul, is it true Dan and Ailsa were once engaged?"

"Where did you get that?" Paul asked incredulously. "They used to date back when Dan was in high school. But his feelings for her were strictly sisterly."

We were interrupted by Bill telephoning. He spoke rapidly in a low voice. "Are you free to talk? I can't leave the paper, but I've found things you should know. You know how I used to fool around with computers in school? I came down to the paper late last night without telling my uncle, and I went hacking on the computer here. I thought those companies that did the land speculation were probably set up right here in Massachusetts, and I was right."

He had a list of all the persons who'd acquired land around Rockcove Hall in the past two years, and some names shook me. One of the Gibbses. Steve. Ailsa. The doctor. Even Detective Simpson. "And a lot of the people went way into debt to do it. I got those figures too. If the developers aren't able to acquire Rockcove Hall, the little people stand to lose their shirts."

The list of suspects had just lengthened.

"Even the police," Paul said bitterly. "I wonder if that's why they were so ready to label the deaths accidents."

"Paul, don't."

"If we only could come up with something definite that would link somebody to the deaths!

Or to Elizabeth's pills, or to the poltergeist. If we knew who it was, we'd know where to look for proof how the things were done."

We ate lunch. The sky was still yellow, but there was no sign of immediate rain. In the afternoon Paul suggested taking the *Sea Witch* around the harbor to survey the terrain from that vantage point. He was restless from inactivity.

"You go. Take Kevin; he'll enjoy it, and you won't have to tell him what you're up to." I glanced at the window and added uneasily, "Be careful."

"I don't kill easily," Paul said. "Especially when I'm forewarned."

They left. I searched for Lissa, and found her sitting out on the point of rocks like a lost water spirit. I went and hugged her. "Darling, don't. Don't be so afraid. Your mother's going to be all right. *Everything* is going to be all right soon." I added after a moment, "I know how the poltergeist tricks were pulled. I know it wasn't you. And they definitely weren't done by thought waves."

She scarcely even heard that. "It's too late to stop anything. Once the Watcher walks—" She stopped, her face going white.

"It isn't the Watcher who's been making appearances on the rocks," I told her. "It was somebody dressing up pretending to be her. Lucinda Lancaster is *not* who you're afraid of. Lissa, I *know*."

Her eyes flared in panic. Then something in my reaction made the panic vanish as fast as it had come. She retreated into that stoic silence, and I knew with a shock that she had already made up her mind Elizabeth would die.

And us too? That was what she was afraid of,

wasn't it? That was what she felt responsible for, and powerless to prevent.

I could say none of this without driving her deeper into terror. Instead, I kissed her, and suggested a visit to the Craig Gallery to see the preview of the works Ailsa would be exhibiting in New York.

I did not realize till I reached the gallery that I was hoping Ailsa would have returned and been there for me to talk to. But she wasn't. An assistant welcomed us pleasantly, and we walked around the open spaces filled with cool gray light. Ailsa's sculpture was part construction, part painting, and part something indefinable. Steel frames were covered with canvas, linen, sheets of metal, paper, and then were painted. Mobiles swung, propelled by some unidentifiable energy source. The colors of some sculptures changed under the impulses of laser beams. It was all very modern, but imbued with the essence of the New England shore.

We went home at last. Paul and Kevin had returned from their coast watch, and Paul greeted me. "How's it going?"

"Not well. . . . Did you find anything?"

He shook his head. "We don't know enough about any of the people. How could anyone have snuck up on Dan, or Asey? At the time Asey had to have died, we were all here. Anyone clambering on the rocks would have been seen. And recognized."

"That could have been the reason for the ghost boat. To run someone into shore without being seen."

"How did they flit around the house playing poltergeist at the same time? What we need is somebody who can be in two places at one time.

And commute between the two places by astral waves."

"What we need is an inventor, like that Mr. Hammond who built the crazy castle."

Then it hit me. I must have changed color; I knew I turned my face away. Because I couldn't voice my realization even to Paul, not yet. But all the same, I knew. And I felt sick.

Paul didn't pick up on it. Thank God, I thought humbly, he isn't psychic. He was staring out the window at the lowering clouds. "I'm going back to the boat," he said abruptly. "And staying there. This is just like the day Dan died. It's just the setting for X to stage the pièce de résistance, and if I'm watching from the water, maybe I can photograph the materialization. Then we'll have our proof."

A prickle ran down my spine as I recalled the grand climaxes warned against in the literature on poltergeists. "Paul—be careful."

"I will. I'll be only as far away as the telephone." There was a cellular phone on the *Sea Witch.* "I'll call you as soon as I see anything," he said, and kissed me, and was gone.

I went to my room and rummaged feverishly through papers until I found the business card Mr. Ikawa had given me. He was a scientist; he worked for an electronics company and had seen the ghost boat. I picked up the phone. If my suspicion was right, there was no need now to worry about anyone listening in from downstairs.

I reached him at his office, apologized for having forgotten to give him his photographs, and told what they had shown. Then I asked my question.

"Yes," Mr. Ikawa said promptly. "Yes, it could be done." I listened carefully as he told me how.

Another piece of circumstantial evidence, but no solid proof.

The afternoon dragged to a close. Ella and I served tea in the Walnut Room for the handful of guests. Mr. Martin came bustling in and announced he was leaving for Maine to visit a friend for a few days, but wanted to retain his room. We all saw him off. We drank tea. We had dinner. I ate early in the kitchen, the children with me. That is, Kevin ate, Lissa merely picked. As quickly as possible she asked to be excused, and vanished. Soon after that, looking from my window, I saw her out on the rocks again, sitting like a statue.

Something cold and tight closed around my heart. I went downstairs to call her in, but a guest stopped me to ask a question about our storm-proofing. By the time I looked out again, Lissa had left the point.

A wind was rising now; the water was full of whitecaps. The storm was coming, and that meant brownout, even without benefit of poltergeist. I got out lots of candles, inspecting them carefully for signs of poltergeist doctoring, and told the guests in the dining room what they could expect. I persuaded them to spend the evening in the TV room, and made it cheerful with plates of cookies, a tray of beverages, and lighted oil lamps. I pointed out the little spinet, and suggested that if the TV blew, someone might feel like playing for a singalong.

Everyone seemed content. I went upstairs.

The main floor and the upper floors were otherwise empty now. I glanced out the window. The

Sea Witch rocked rhythmically at her mooring, all in darkness. I looked into Lissa's room, but it was empty. I went back to my own rooms to wait, my ears straining. At last I heard the sound of footsteps on the stairs.

I ran through my sitting room to the door and threw it open. "Lissa!"

There was no one in the hall. But the faint sound continued. Stopped. Lissa's door was locked. I had a key. I unlocked the door swiftly and pushed it in.

Lissa was there in her window seat, hugging her knees.

"How did you get in here?" She didn't answer, and I ran and shook her. "There are stairs in the walls, aren't there? That's how you do your disappearing acts. That's how the poltergeist has gotten around. I don't care what promises you've made, you *must* tell me!"

Twenty-four

Lissa's eyes flared. "I can't!"

"You can! You took an oath of some kind, didn't you? That's what you meant when you told me once that Asey talked too much, and then he died. When you kept telling me I didn't understand. You meant they—we—are *causing* the things that happen. A—a kind of retribution because we wish things, see things, pry into things where we shouldn't!"

Her eyes were terrified. I longed to sweep her into my arms, but I had to keep her eyes on mine. "Lissa, I *know*. All of it—almost all. Because I—know the Watcher too. Not the imposter on the rocks. The real one. She's here with us now. You know that, don't you?"

The currents in the room grew warm and thrummed. Lissa's eyes lost some of their look of fear.

"Her name was Lucinda Clayborne. *I'm* a Lucinda Clayborne. I think I've been—called here this summer so she can work through me. That first Lucinda died because someone she trusted played a trick on her—a murderous trick. Your father died that way too. And Asey. Your mother almost died. And the Watcher... saw it coming, and was powerless to prevent it... unless we helped her. That's the way it's been for you, hasn't it? You've seen—things. And you've been powerless. But you don't have to stay that way now. You mustn't."

Lissa was starting to shake. A tear rolled down her cheek. "Lissa," I said gently, "something's going to happen tonight. Both of us know it. If you don't tell me what you know, I may be killed. And then who will protect your mother?"

She looked back at me, and I saw her come to a decision before she spoke. "I saw... the ghost boat force the *Sea Witch* onto the rocks... that night."

The thrumming in the room intensified. I held my breath. After a moment Lissa went on, so quietly. "That night... I heard Daddy go out, and I was scared. I felt the Watcher warning me, and I... I sneaked out, to try to stop him. Only I couldn't. Daddy was already in the dory, heading for the *Sea Witch*, and the storm was so loud, he couldn't hear me. So I sat down on the rocks to wait for him to come home."

The picture rose vividly before my eyes. The small boat, battling the elements at Dan Lancaster's dogged command; the small figure watching, battered by wind and rain.

Lissa continued. "He lit the lights on the *Sea Witch*, and he got her started. He was just turning her out toward open water when the—the ghost boat was there. Just a small one. Headed right for the *Sea Witch*. Daddy tried to turn out of the way, but the little boat kept coming. It was forcing the

Sea Witch straight toward the rocks . . . . Daddy jumped off the side. He must have hit his head. He just lay there. And then *she* was there. . . ."

I knew whom she meant. I could almost see the figure in the copper dress materializing from the rocks, bending over the unconscious man. Then on a sudden impulse, lifting a rock, and bringing it down. . . .

So Dan's death had not been premeditated as Asey's had been. The intention had been what? To delay him? To persuade him?

"She didn't see me at first." Lissa halted for a moment. "Then she came past me. I heard her dress rustle. And she turned, and saw. . ." She closed her eyes briefly, but the young unchildlike voice went on. "She said my father had not kept faith. Just like that old Captain Lancaster years ago. And that I must—promise never to tell what I had seen, or she—she would come again. And whenever she came, there would be another death. So I promised."

She was talking now, deliberately accepting what she felt would be her doom, to spare me—My throat was tight.

"She comes in and out through the walls, doesn't she? Just as you've done. That's why she hasn't been seen. I found a passage from the shore to the carriage house, but there are others too. There's one in the wall here, isn't there?"

In answer Lissa went to her closet and pressed a knothole. The side wall pivoted, revealing a staircase, a duplicate of the one out in the hall. They probably had common stair treads. I started to go down it, but she stopped me.

"It goes to the cellar. Next to the TV room. You

can get into there by a panel underneath the lower stairs. There's a passage into Mom's room too. From the attic, to the room above, and then on down to the Walnut Room. And then there's one from there to the carriage house."

In other words, the ghost could get in and out of Rockcove Hall at any time, unseen.

The thrumming in the room grew stronger. I could almost feel Lucinda's hand upon my shoulder. But there was no urgency to her yet. Only a deep relief and a coiled waiting.

"She said death came to Rockcove Hall by foot, by water, and by fire," Lissa said. Her voice was not her own.

"Whichever way anything comes tonight, it won't reach us. Paul's in the *Sea Witch*, watching. He'll warn us the moment he sees it approaching, and he'll phone the police."

Lissa accepted this, but it did not comfort her.

I persuaded her to go to sleep in my room, and I lay down with her. First I changed, not into my nightgown, but into a shirt and jeans. I would be prepared for anything. "Lissa," I said gently, "I know why you need a light, now, but tonight they must be out. You know that, don't you?"

She nodded.

We lay down, but we did not sleep. The hours ticked by. Outside the windows lightning crackled suddenly. The *Sea Witch* rolled on the rocky water resolutely. Then came the rain.

It came in a flood, roaring down the eaves and drainpipes. There was no mist outside, but I could see little. Yet I had absolute faith that Paul would see the ghost's approach. It would come by phantom boat, as in that other storm, probably.

There was a creak in the wall beside my bed. I could feel all Lissa's senses tense and grow alert. And then I heard it. The sound, so infinitesimal, that I had recognized for the first time, earlier, as a footstep on a stair tread in the wall.

The intruder wasn't coming by foot or sea. The intruder was already here. Had been here, perhaps, all along...

The steps climbed upward, moved across the ceiling in the attic crawl space, and disappeared in the direction of the hall's central core. I knew suddenly where they were going.

I reached for the telephone to call Paul, and the line was dead. Down? Cut? It scarcely mattered. Paul must be told, and quickly. I swung round to Lissa.

"You'll have to get Paul. Swim to the *Sea Witch*, or take the boat, whichever you want." Thank God, she could swim like a fish and run an outboard! "Lissa, you have to. Paul's shortwave phone will get the police. Tell him the poltergeist is heading for the main attic, and he must come!"

She was out of bed like a cat, running down the hidden stairs in her slippers and brief pajamas.

I slid my feet into flat Chinese slippers and grabbed the flashlight and set of keys I had held ready. I let myself out into the corridor. The whole house slumbered. Wake the guests to escape? No, it would take too much time. I had to reach her first, and prevent what was coming.

By water, and by fire.

Then I was in the main hall; I was running soundlessly to the third floor. The attic door was bolted. Naturally. She'd left it open those other times for sheer torture; she herself moved through walls.

Up to the attic. It was empty. I knew that by sensing, by the quality of the vibrations I was receiving from the guardian spirit that moved beside me. Then the ladder-stairs to the widow's walk, and the trapdoor. That would be tricky. She might see me open it, or hear a creak.

God was with me. The trapdoor was already open.

I was up onto the widow's walk, and she had not even heard me in the noises of the storm. Her back was to me as she stared out toward the shoreline, her hair wet and whipping in the wind. I had to call her to make her turn.

"Ailsa!"

She swung around then, one hand clutched against her raincoat at her chest. Not to keep the coat closed; no. Something small and metallic glittered on her fingers.

"So you knew who it was." Her eyes mocked me. "I was afraid you were intelligent. You're so much like Elizabeth, but she's soft." Her voice held contempt.

"That's why Dan chose her though," I said quietly. "That's why Steve did too. You love Steve, and Elizabeth took him, just as she'd taken Dan."

That was not the literal truth, but my only hope was to keep her talking until help came.

It was working for the moment. "You think you know it all, don't you?" she taunted.

"I know most of it. You loved Steve, and so you tried to persuade Dan not to prosecute him. It had to be you Dan went to see that night. Somebody very close to him, somebody he could trust, and who cared for Steve as he did. Only Dan had the Lancaster temper, and he was determined to see Steve and—what? Make him turn himself over to the police?"

"Steve's soft too," Ailsa said coolly. "And weak. Not like Dan was. But I did love him. I knew how to manage him, and I couldn't let Dan ruin him."

"So you sent a boat out by remote control to chase Dan," I said steadily. "I figured that out after seeing your gallery show. You know all about engineering, and electronics, and electricity. That was why you were able to work the poltergeist stunts. It didn't matter to you that Lissa felt herself to blame. All that mattered by then was getting even with Elizabeth. And covering your murder. Murders, because you killed Asey too. Because he saw you. What were you going to do about Lissa? And now me? Drown us too?"

I knew that was not what she had in mind, but I had to goad her into taking the remote control device away from her chest. Because somewhere in the hall, there was a bomb.

Distantly I heard the sound of an outboard plowing toward the shore. Headlights swept down the road. Ailsa did not see them. Her eyes narrowed, and her arm swept up and out.

I dove at her. I grabbed the arm with the device and the two of us struggled, wrestled, until the device fell from her hand and rolled harmlessly down the roof.

Ailsa screamed. Her shriek was the shriek of the dead, and she leaned over the railing of the widow's walk, groping, reaching.

With another, different shriek, the old Chippendale railing gave way. I tried to reach her, to grab her back. As God is my witness, I did try. But it was no use. Ailsa plunged over the railing, over the roof, to crash onto the stones of the terrace far below.

That was where Paul and Lissa and the police found her, lying like a broken doll.

Twenty-five

"It's hard to believe," Elizabeth said slowly, "that she hated me that much."

It was the day after Labor Day, and all our guests were gone. Elizabeth had just come home from the hospital, where the doctor had insisted on keeping her till the tourist season ended. The police had interviewed her there more than once, and Paul and I had paid her visits, but this was the first chance the three of us had had to really talk. Kevin and Lissa were being kept outdoors by Martha Gibbs. It was late afternoon; Elizabeth was back in the big bedroom that had been hers and Dan's, looking frail but clear-eyed. Paul and I were having tea with her and talking, talking... trying to make sense out of irrational tragedy.

"I can't believe Ailsa could have hated us that much," Elizabeth repeated. "She was Dan's cousin. She was my best friend."

"She didn't hate *us*," Paul said. "It was you, personally. Ailsa may have been family, but her feelings for Dan were anything but cousinly. She must have resented you for years because he fell for you. And she sure as hell resented you for taking McGovern away from her too!"

We were silent for a moment. We all knew, now, that both Steve and Ailsa had been investing in real estate around Rockcove Hall under the names of dummy corporations. Steve had been hoping to replace the money missing from Dan's estate; Ailsa had been hoping to make money, period—after Elizabeth sold Rockcove Hall to the developers so the shopping mall could be built.

We also knew it had been Ailsa, so close to both Dan and Steve, whom Dan had called first that night he died. Ailsa, whom Dan had told of his suspicions and his decision to confront Steve with them. Ailsa, who had told Dan the roads were closed, thus forcing him to take the *Sea Witch* out. Ailsa, who loved Steve passionately, and who had come to the cove in a boat she could direct by remote control... who had sent that boat out like a ghost to force the *Sea Witch* into land... and who had then killed Dan. To keep the man she once had loved from bringing shame, disgrace, perhaps jail to the man whom she loved now.

The police knew that now too. Probably all Cape Ann did. Steve had spent considerable time with the police, but he was not in jail. He had also paid a long visit to Elizabeth in the hospital, following Ailsa's death. Neither Paul nor I knew what had taken place, and we dared not ask. And Elizabeth was talking, not of Steve, but Ailsa.

"The police brought her diary for me to read. There were things in it they needed me to clear up." Elizabeth shook her head. "She must have been mad. That's the only explanation that makes sense."

"Maybe she was at the end. She sure knew what she was doing when she rigged that accident for Dan, and when she killed Asey," Paul said.

"And when she rigged the poltergeist, and all the other manifestations," I said, and shivered. It had all been spelled out in the dairy, and Elizabeth and Paul and I were fitting the facts together like the pieces of a jigsaw puzzle.

Phone calls, that was one group of pieces. Ailsa on the phone with Dan the night he died. Ailsa calling CJG developers, pretending to be Elizabeth, saying she'd decided to sell the hall. Ailsa doing the heavy-breathing bit to frighten me off. Ailsa phoning an invitation for Bill to the newspaper the night of the whaling-days dinner, so the "press" would be on hand for the poltergeist's first appearance.

Poltergeist, that had been another group of pieces. If I hated Ailsa for nothing else, I would for that: creating malevolent manifestations of the Watcher to scare the inn guests off, and doing it in a way that suspicion would rest on Lissa.

The Watcher—that was another piece. Ailsa dressing up as Lucinda Clayborne Lancaster and "materializing" to scare people, to silence Lissa. Ailsa herself, slipping like a ghost through the rooms and grounds she knew so well; slipping through the hidden passages to commit murder.

"There really was a Watcher here all summer," I said aloud.

"She was trying to warn us. But you wouldn't listen." Lissa had come in, as silent as a ghost. No one told her to leave. Elizabeth held out an arm to her and Lissa went to sit beside her, her face sober. "The Watcher didn't want to hurt us. *You* know that," Lissa said, looking straight at me.

I smiled at her in silent covenant, but what I said was, "I meant Ailsa. Now that I look back, Ailsa was always here. Always watching." I caught my breath. "That's why the really dangerous things started happening, wasn't it? Because Ailsa was here and heard Steve ask Elizabeth to marry him. Up till then . . . the accidents to Rockcove Hall, the phone calls, the poltergeist. . ." I looked at Elizabeth. "She did them to try to force you to sell the hall and go away. So the shopping mall would be built. So you wouldn't find out the truth about Dan's death and Dan's money; so you'd be away from Steve. But after Steve proposed, she wanted you dead."

Elizabeth nodded. "That's exactly what her diary said. She couldn't bear the idea that her closest friend was again taking away a man she loved." She was silent for a moment, gazing sadly at a picture of Ailsa on the bureau. "The ice maiden. That's what we called her in college. So cool and imperturbable on the surface, all that obsessive passion bottled in. It must have unbalanced her. That's the kindest explanation."

I did not feel kind. I crossed to the bureau and deliberately tore the photograph into little pieces and dropped them in the basket.

"That won't get rid of her," Lissa said gravely. Elizabeth hugged her.

"No, it won't. But it made Cindy feel better, I imagine. Someday we'll all be able to remember without pain. You will, too, darling, and that's important. Good's stronger than evil, even in the grave. The vibes at Rockcove Hall are good ones, and all our ghosts are kind."

"The Watcher." Paul groaned, though his eyes were tender. "Haven't we had enough of the supernatural for a while? Can't you women ever let it rest?"

I just smiled, and after a moment so did Lissa. There were some things that didn't need discussing, at least not now. Like the Watcher, and her kinship with me. Like Steve McGovern's relationship—past, present, future—with Elizabeth. She apparently wasn't pressing legal charges against him for mismanagement of Dan's funds. Whether things would ever go back to their old footing, I did not presume to guess. Stranger things had happened. Look at Paul and me, I thought, and smiled.

None of that, happily, had gotten into print. I'll tell my mother about it, I thought. Someday. Right now it was time for life to get back to normal. Elizabeth was recovering. Rockcove Hall would continue as Lancaster property, and flourish as an inn. Paul would go back to college. Further than that into the future I would not look.

"Anyway"—Paul voiced what we all were thinking—"it's over now. Thank the Lord!"

Elizabeth's eyes twinkled. "I really didn't think you'd be all that glad to have summer over. You have to hit the books again. Cindy goes home tomorrow."

"Cindy," Paul said firmly, "is a part of this place. Forever."

And he reached for me, and took me in his arms, and kissed me. Paul, the strong and silent, the undemonstrative, kissing me before an audience of relatives. A lot of things have changed this summer, I thought dizzily when he released me.

As far as Rockport was concerned, of course, everything was simply back to normal. The mystery surrounding Rockcove Hall was solved, all I's dotted and T's crossed. If there were a lot of other letters in the alphabet as yet unrevealed, that was family business.

Those glass spheres, for example. They still rested on my bureau, faintly tinted, faintly glimmering with gold. If Rockport assumed I'd found them in the attic, let them. If I chose to believe they'd come to me as talismans from a Watcher in the mist, that was my privilege. I didn't have to tell skeptics. I knew what I knew.

I would probably tell Elizabeth, who would not laugh. I did not have to tell Lissa, who had seen the Watcher too.

But one distant day, one special day, I *would* tell Paul.

ABOUT THE AUTHOR

NORMA JOHNSTON is the author of over sixty books for adults and young adults, including the Carlisle Chronicles series for Bantam Starfire Books and the acclaimed Keeping Days series. Ms. Johnston has traveled extensively around the world, and at various times has been a teacher, actress, play director, boutique owner, and free-lance editor. She is currently at work on *Shadow of a Unicorn*, another mystery to be published as a Bantam Starfire Book.

The Carlisle Chronicles

Three tales of the Carlisle Family starring 15-year-old Jess Carlisle

Jess Carlisle's father works for the government and the family has moved around a lot. Maybe that's why roots and "family" are so important to her—she's the only Carlisle who doesn't enjoy being footloose.

☐ **CARLISLE'S HOPE: CARLISLE CHRONICLES #1** 25467 $2.50/2.95 in Canada
When she delves into Carlisle family history for a school project, Jess uncovers an old secret that forever changes the way she views her family, and herself.

☐ **TO JESS WITH LOVE AND MEMORIES: CARLISLE CHRONICLES #2** 25882 $2.50
When Jess discovers she was adopted, she reacts with bitterness and hurt, until she learns the real truth about her birth.

CARLISLE'S ALL: CARLISLE CHRONICLES #3. *Coming in November.*
Mr. Carlisle's taken hostage in the Middle East and the Carlisle's must all pull together to find a way to free him.

Order CARLISLE'S HOPE: CARLISLE CHRONICLES #1 now.

FOR JESS WITH LOVE AND MEMORIES: CARLISLE CHRONICLES #2

Watch for:

CARLISLE'S ALL: CARLISLE CHRONICLES #3
Coming in November.

Bantam Books, Inc., Dept. DA14, 414 East Golf Road, Des Plaines, Ill. 60016

Please send me the books I have checked above. I am enclosing $_____ (please add $1.50 to cover postage and handling. Send check or money order—no cash or C.O.D.'s please).

Mr/Mrs/Miss _____

Address _____

City/State _____ Zip _____

DA14—9/86
Please allow four to six weeks for delivery. This offer expires 3/87.

Stories of Love
That Will Live Forever

BANTAM
SHOP·AT·HOME
C·A·T·A·L·O·G

Special Offer
Buy a Bantam Book
for only 50¢.

Now you can order the exciting books you've been wanting to read straight from Bantam's latest listing of hundreds of titles. *And* this special offer gives you the opportunity to purchase a Bantam book for only 50¢. Here's how:

By ordering any five books at the regular price per order, you can also choose any other single book listed (up to $4.95 value) for only 50¢. Some restrictions do apply, so for further details send for Bantam's listing of titles today.

Just send us your name and address and we'll send you Bantam Book's SHOP AT HOME CATALOG!